Coup de Glace

Also by this Author

Mystery/Suspense:

Auntie Clem's Bakery
Gluten-Free Murder
Dairy-Free Death
Allergen-Free Assignation
Witch-Free Halloween (Halloween Short)
Dog-Free Dinner (Christmas Short)
Stirring Up Murder
Brewing Death
Coup de Glace

Zachary Goldman Mysteries
She Wore Mourning
His Hands Were Quiet (Coming Soon)
She Was Dying Anyway (Coming Soon)
He was Walking Alone (Coming Soon)

Looking Over Your Shoulder
Lion Within
Pursued by the Past
In the Tick of Time
Loose the Dogs

Cowritten with D. D. VanDyke
California Corwin P. I. Mystery Series
The Girl in the Morgue

Young Adult Fiction:

Between the Cracks:
Ruby
June and Justin
Michelle
Chloe
Ronnie

Tamara's Teardrops:
Tattooed Teardrops
Two Teardrops
Tortured Teardrops
Vanishing Teardrops

Breaking the Pattern:
Deviation
Diversion
By-Pass

Stand Alone
Don't Forget Steven
Those Who Believe
Cynthia has a Secret
Questing for a Dream
Once Brothers
Intersexion
Making Her Mark
Endless Change

Coupe de Glace

Auntie Clem's Bakery
Book 6

P.D. Workman

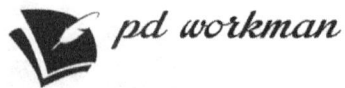

Copyright © 2018 P.D. Workman

All rights reserved. No part of this publication may be reproduced, stored in retrieval system, copied in any form or by any means, electronic, mechanical, photocopying, recording or otherwise transmitted without written permission from the publisher. You must not circulate this book in any format.

ISBN: 9781989080382

To an unflinching look at the past.

Chapter One

IT WAS HARD FOR Erin to believe that Bella and Vic were only a year apart in age, if that. Vic was her own woman, independent, knowledgeable, opinionated. Sometimes Erin felt like Vic was older than she herself. But Bella was definitely still a kid. Having graduated from high school, she was available to help out at the bakery more often, but Erin had a hard time thinking of her as a grown up.

Vic had taken the day off to go into the city with Willie. Erin was glad to see them back together again, working through their differences. There was still tension between them, not over Vic's transgender identity, but over the recent revelations of Willie's past and that he had kept back from Vic the fact that they were from opposing sides of a generations-long clan war. He'd known about it from the start, but had kept his involvement with the Dyson organized crime family from her.

Despite Vic's feelings about the deception, they had made up and were trying to get back on track again. A day away from Bald Eagle Falls would be good for them. It was easy to get caught up in the personalities of the small Tennessee town and to forget that things were not the same everywhere. Going somewhere else provided a little perspective. Vic had never been outside of Tennessee, and Erin hoped that someday she'd travel a little and broaden her horizons. As long as she still came back to Auntie

COUP DE GLACE

Clem's Bakery when she was done. Erin wanted Vic to grow, but didn't know what she'd do without her.

"Erin, can we make more of the gumdrop cookies and put chocolate chips in them?"

Erin was pulled from her ponderings. She looked at Bella, blinking to refocus herself.

"They're not gumdrop cookies if you use chocolate chips," she pointed out.

"Unless you put gumdrops and chocolate chips in them…"

Erin considered the suggestion. Chocolate and gumdrops. Erin's gumdrop cookies were pretty popular, but she'd never considered including both chocolate chips and gumdrops.

"That's an interesting idea. Do you think people would go for them?"

Bella's blue eyes twinkled. "You can't wreck something by adding chocolate to it!" Her curly blond hair was pulled back from her round face, making her look younger than her seventeen years.

Erin laughed. "Okay, we can give it a try. Substitute part of the gumdrops with chocolate chips, and we'll call them 'Bella's Dream' cookies."

"Can't we just add chocolate chips?"

"You have to have enough cookie dough for them to hold together, especially with gluten-free cookies. If you increase the add-ins too much, they'll just fall apart into a crumbly mess when you try to pick them up."

"Oh." Bella nodded. "That makes sense."

She got out the gumdrops and the chocolate chips and measured them into her cookie batter before turning the mixer on. "It's too bad we can't use peanuts," she said. "My mom makes these awesome Reese's Pieces and chocolate chip cookies. They are *so* good!"

"I'll bet they are," Erin agreed. "I like anything with chocolate and peanut butter. But no peanuts or nuts in

Auntie Clem's Bakery. They are too common an allergen and I don't want even the possibility of cross-contamination."

"I know." Bella let out a sigh. "Your baking is really good, but sometimes I wish we could just do normal cooking and not have to worry about allergies and Celiac disease and all that."

"Imagine how you would feel if you had a life-threatening condition that meant you couldn't ever eat those things," Erin said. "It isn't easy going through life not being able to eat what you want. You and I can just go home and make Reese's Pieces cookies if we feel like it. Someone with an allergy can't. They just have to forgo it forever." Erin made a motion to encompass the baking they were each working on. "That's why we do this. So that people with allergies or intolerances can have some variety. If people without dietary restrictions want something that's not gluten- or allergen-free, they can just go into the city or make their own. It isn't so easy for someone with a life-threatening condition."

Bella nodded. She took a deep sniff of the cookie dough. "I'm sure glad that I can eat whatever I want. Although..." she patted her stomach, "I probably shouldn't eat it all!"

Erin just shrugged. She was careful not to eat too much of her own baking, but she didn't struggle with it like Bella. Bella had been overweight before working at Auntie Clem's and, while not obese, she had put on a few more pounds since starting.

"I might just have to go out and buy some Reese's Pieces after work," Bella said. "Now I'm going to be craving them all day."

"Have you ever seen *E.T.*?" Erin asked, trying to distract Bella from thoughts about the candy. "That is such a good show."

COUP DE GLACE

Bella shuddered. "No. One of my friends tried to put it on once, but it was so spooky, and I was really freaked out. I don't like movies about creepy aliens."

"But he's not creepy. He's just different. He's really lovable and funny."

"I couldn't get past the first five minutes." Bella shook her head. "No way, you can keep your supernatural stuff."

Erin shook her head and folded raisins into the muffin batter she was working on.

"I know," Bella said. "I'm a scaredy-cat about everything. I should grow up and act like an adult instead of a baby."

"I never said that. There are plenty of adults who are afraid of… supernatural things. It doesn't make you a baby."

"Most adults aren't afraid of everything that goes bump in the night. I wish I wasn't."

"Maybe you could see a psychologist or something. Someone who could help you to get over it. They have programs to help people overcome phobias and anxieties."

"No. I've been to them before. They never really help. They always want you to confront your fears. Desensitize yourself. I just… can't."

"So how are you supposed to do that? Watch scary movies?"

Erin expected Bella to laugh, but she didn't. She shook her head, face pale. "No…"

There was silence for a few minutes, Erin not sure what to say.

"They want me to go into the barn," Bella said.

"Into the barn? What barn?"

"At home. There's an old barn. It's… haunted."

Erin laughed. But Bella wasn't kidding. Her lips tightened. She was over-mixing the cookie dough, not paying attention to what she was doing.

"It is! I know you don't believe in ghosts, but that doesn't mean you're right. You wouldn't say that if you'd seen some of the weird stuff I have. That old barn really is haunted."

"Okay." Erin held up her hands. "I'm sorry. I shouldn't have laughed. You just caught me by surprise. You've never mentioned your haunted barn before."

Bella eyed her as if suspicious that Erin was making fun of her. She turned off her mixer and pulled out a couple of cookie sheets.

"It's never come up before."

"Do you know… who it's haunted by?" Erin asked tentatively. She wasn't sure whether that was the appropriate thing to do. Was it polite to ask people about their haunted outbuildings? Or was that a taboo topic?

Bella nodded. "My grandma." She started to scoop the cookie dough out onto the tray, carefully spacing the cookies apart so they wouldn't spread into each other.

"Oh."

Erin started pouring out the muffins. When she looked up, Bella was watching her intently, and Erin wondered if she'd missed part of the conversation while focused on the job at hand.

"You could help me! You're really good at solving mysteries. If you solved Grandma's murder, then maybe she'd stop haunting the barn, and I wouldn't have to be scared of going near there anymore."

Erin smiled and shook her head. "I'm a baker, not a detective."

"You haven't always been a baker, though. You've done all kinds of other things."

"I've done other things. But I'm not a private investigator or policeman and I never have been."

"But you've solved other mysteries. Lots of them."

COUP DE GLACE

"Just... lucky. Terry doesn't want me to get involved in any more police stuff. Not that I want to. It's always just fallen into my lap before."

"Officer Handsome can't control what you do. And if you were looking into a really old case, then it's not like you'd be in any danger, right?"

Erin grinned at Bella calling Terry Piper 'Officer Handsome.' He was that! Especially when he smiled at her and that little dimple appeared in his cheek. A lot of the Bald Eagles Falls women sighed over Officer Piper in uniform, patrolling and investigating with his canine partner at his side. He and Erin had known each other for almost a year and, while it hadn't been a whirlwind romance, things had progressed, and she did catch herself thinking of him as belonging to her, even though they weren't engaged and hadn't ever talked about an exclusive relationship.

"It's not just Terry. I don't really want to get involved in another mystery. The ones I've been involved with before now... Things have not always had a happy ending."

Bella nodded her understanding, but she wasn't ready to let the matter drop. "But like I said, this is a really old case. My grandpa isn't around anymore. No one would be trying to stop you from finding out the truth. There wouldn't be any danger, to you or anyone else."

"Just because it's an old case, that doesn't mean no one cares about it anymore." Erin was thinking about Bertie Braceling. "Sometimes, people get so caught up in trying to protect the past... people's reputations... histories that they've rewritten... what happened years ago still has an effect on today. Trust me."

"Okay." Bella sighed. "I guess I understand why you're scared to look into it."

The word *scared* irritated Erin. She wasn't scared. She was just cautious. She just didn't see the point in getting involved in something that wasn't any of her business. In the past, she'd had to get involved in cases because she or her friends had been the prime suspects. She didn't have any vested interest in what had happened to Bella's grandmother.

Bella picked up the cookie trays to put them into the ovens.

"Put them in the fridge for a few minutes first," Erin advised. "I think the dough might have warmed up too much. They'll spread too much and burn."

Bella considered the cookies for a moment, looking like she was going to argue, then nodded. "Okay." She took them to the fridge as instructed.

"It would just be really nice to be able to go to my own barn," she said with a shrug.

Erin wasn't so sure that solving her grandmother's murder would help Bella to go into the barn. She still couldn't go to the commode in the basement of Auntie Clem's bakery, even though Angela Plaint's murder had been solved and the loo was not haunted. Bella was still convinced that it was and refused to use the facilities. It was irritating to Erin that Bella couldn't retrieve any supplies from the storeroom and had to go down the street if she needed to use the toilet during her shift.

Chapter Two

FROM HER ATTIC READING room, Erin looked out the window to the loft over the garage, but there were no lights on. Vic and Willie had not yet returned. Vic had Sunday off as well; she and Willie could spend the night in the city or somewhere other than the loft apartment. While Willie had spent the night with Vic in the past, it had been when she had needed protection, and Vic had made it clear that they were not intimate. Erin didn't quite understand Vic's moral standards or why she cared if anyone thought she and Willie were sleeping together, but she just shrugged it off as part of what made Vic unique.

"Looks like it's just you and me tonight," Erin told Orange Blossom, the ginger cat who sat waiting for her to settle somewhere. "And Marshmallow, of course." She hadn't brought the rabbit up to run around and play with Blossom, nervous that he would fall down the stairs.

She picked up Clementine's previously missing journal, found in the deceased Joelle Biggs's possessions, and decided on the window seat. She sat down and patted the cushion beside her for Orange Blossom to jump up. He did so immediately, purr-meowing at her and chattering on about his day. It took a few minutes for him to find a comfortable position, kneading her thighs with his needle-sharp claws.

"Come on, Blossom…"

He finally settled and was still, purring his loud happy rumble. Erin opened up the journal. It was the one that

Clementine had been writing when Erin's parents had been killed, and Erin was curious about what Clementine had known of the car accident that had left Erin an orphan and the intrigue that surrounded it.

To begin with, the mentions of her parents were general, "I have called Luke and Kathryn repeatedly, to no avail," and "Still no word from Luke." She obviously hadn't known about the accident right away. As far as she knew, her brother and his family had just gone away and refused to have anything to do with her. It sounded from Clementine's outpourings that she had perhaps had words with Erin's father about their parenting and the instability in Erin's life, and Clementine thought he was upset with her because of their argument.

There were also mentions of the Plaint boys. She hadn't known they'd had anything to do with her brother's disappearance, but she was clearly concerned about Davis. His descent into depression and drug use had not gone unnoticed. She had caught him squatting in the summer house that was now Adele's home, and had to send him on his way.

> I couldn't let Davis hang around on the property, especially to crash at the summer house. I don't need teenagers or drifters setting up house there, running it down. I told him he needed to leave and not trespass on my property. If he needs something, he's welcome to come to the house. I'm more than happy to give him work, food, or just a listening ear.

Erin rubbed her eyes, telling herself they were burning because she was tired. What Davis had gone through because of his father's bad choices... even Trenton had suffered. He might have been a bully and a jock, but he hadn't been untouched by his father's unfaithfulness and his death. Adam Plaint might have thought that no one was being hurt by his affairs, but they had all been affected for decades to come.

Clementine had tried to reach out in kindness to Davis, even though she hadn't known the full extent of what he had been through. She had seen that he was hurting and had tried to offer him some kind of support.

"You missed your dad too, didn't you, Davis?" Erin murmured.

Orange Blossom raised his head to look at Erin, then decided she wasn't talking to him and put it back down to nap. Erin read on, trying not to get mired down in her own history. Yes, she missed her dad, and her mom too. But it had been twenty years and she wasn't a kid anymore. Sure, her childhood had sucked, passed from one foster home to another, yet life went on. She had worked hard and made something of herself.

The inheritance of Clementine's house and shop had made it possible for her to become her own boss, something she hadn't ever known if she would be able to do. So far, she was doing well, making a living at Auntie Clem's Bakery. Without the bakery, Erin would still have been trapped in dead-end jobs and Vic might have been out on the street.

But Clementine had more to report on than just her absent brother and the troubles of the Plaint boys. Erin's brow furrowed as she read on.

> Strange happenings over at the Prost farm. I know that Ezekiel and Martha have always been strange ducks, but this is stranger than usual. Rumor has it that Martha has passed away, but Ezekiel will not let anyone into the house to see. He insists that she's just fine and will call them back later. But no one has gotten a call back from her and people are quite sure she's dead. The sheriff is seeing what he can do about getting in there, but apparently there is not much he can do if he doesn't have any evidence there has been a crime committed or

that anyone is in immediate danger. Martha isn't in danger if she is dead, and Ezekiel wouldn't be guilty of anything other than misleading people and maybe improper disposal of a body if he's done something with her.

That was certainly an eye-opener. Another mysterious death or disappearance in Bald Eagle Falls? Even stranger, Erin had read through all of the newspapers around the time of her parents' deaths, and there had been nothing in the local weekly about a Martha Prost dying or disappearing under mysterious circumstances. That would certainly have caught Erin's attention.

But maybe it had just been a rumor. Probably, Martha had shown up again, perfectly healthy and happy, just like her husband said she would, and the rumor of her death was just that, a rumor, with nothing to back it.

Erin looked out the window toward Vic's loft again. She should have noticed if the light had been turned on, but she had been deeply interested in what she was reading. The apartment was still dark.

"I don't think she's going to make it back tonight," Erin told Orange Blossom. "They must be having too good a time."

Blossom sat up and yowled at her, a long, mournful sound that he made when she left him alone or took him in the car to the vet. Erin laughed and scratched his ears.

"We'll be fine if she stays away overnight. She doesn't sleep in the house anymore anyway."

Erin yawned, scrubbed at her eyes again, and decided it must be more than the dust from the journal that was making her eyes feel gritty. She needed to be up early in the morning for the bakery. Not as early as usual, because it would be Sunday, which was just the ladies' tea, and she didn't have to have everything baked that she would on a regular day. Just a few cookies and treats and an assortment of teas at the ready for when the women got out of their church services.

"It's my one night to sleep in," she told the cat, "I'd better take advantage of it."

Chapter Three

THINGS WENT WELL AT the ladies' tea. It was pretty routine after a year, with no unexpected bumps in the road. Erin and Bella were cleaning up when Erin heard the jingling of the bells at the front door. She had a pretty good idea who it would be. Everyone knew that the tea would be over, and she would be closed. Erin looked out the kitchen doorway to the front of the shop.

"Come on in," she invited Officer Terry Piper.

He locked the front door for her and walked around the counter and through the kitchen door to join them. K9 panted at Terry's side.

"Do you want some water?" Erin suggested. "As Vic would say, it's almighty hot out there."

"Vic would not," Terry countered, "since this is still pretty mild for late spring."

"Fine, then *I'll* say it's almighty hot. Does K9 want a drink?"

Terry looked down at his partner.

"I'm sure he does," he agreed. "And a cookie. But you go ahead," he motioned toward the sink, "you finish cleaning up. I know where everything is."

Erin would protest that he didn't have to serve himself, but if she let him do it, she would be out of there all that much earlier. She shrugged. "Okay. Let me know if you need a hand with anything."

Erin went back to work and Terry got himself and K9 water and a cookie each. K9 seemed just as happy with his

COUP DE GLACE

doggie biscuit as Terry was with his Bella's Dream cookie. Terry walked into the kitchen munching on it.

"Great idea, Bella," he told the girl, toasting her with the cookie. "I love them."

Bella turned pink and fanned herself with her hand. "Thank you, Officer Piper!"

"I'll be happy to test new combinations for you anytime."

Erin looked over at him. "Charley suggested that we try crickets in the protein bars."

A little wrinkle appeared between Terry's eyebrows. "Crickets? Is that some nickname for some kind of dried fruit or seed?"

"Nope. Crickets. Like she feeds to Iggy."

Terry made a face. "Don't even talk to me about crickets while eating. And remind me not to try anything labeled high protein if she ever reopens The Bake Shoppe. I'm not going to be *her* guinea pig."

"They are supposed to be very good for you. Low in fat."

"Well, so are a lot of things I don't intend to eat."

"K9 would eat them, wouldn't you, boy?"

K9 looked up at Erin with a little whine. They all laughed. They finished the clean-up together and Erin was free for the afternoon.

"Do you need a ride?" Terry asked Bella, as Erin locked the back door.

Bella shook her head. "No, it's okay. My mom is picking me up. She'll be here any minute."

"You're sure? Call Erin if you get stranded and we'll come back for you."

Bella waved him off. "I'm fine. Mom's coming."

Erin and Terry left her waiting in the back parking lot. They got into Erin's car; Erin knew his would be at the police department and they could pick it up later.

"Everything quiet this morning?" Erin asked.

"Like a Sunday morning in a small town."

Erin looked in her rear-view mirror at Bella. "Are you worried about her? Did you want to wait?"

"No, she'll be fine. I'm surprised she doesn't have a car of her own. Doesn't she have a license?"

"I don't think so. Her mom strikes me as a little… overprotective. She probably doesn't want Bella to be driving around on her own."

"Most kids out in the country are driving as soon as they are fourteen and have their licenses and their own cars as soon as they can. No parent wants to be driving around all over the county with them."

"I've noticed. I see kids who look like they're barely out of kindergarten with their own cars. I had my license when I was eighteen, but I didn't have enough money to get my own vehicle yet. And when I did have money to get my own…" Erin patted the steering wheel of the Challenger, "it was always a beater."

"With Bella living out of town, I would have thought she would have her own little beater by now. Maybe she's saving up for one."

Erin nodded, but secretly she wondered about Bella's mother. Erin hadn't seen Cindy very often, usually just a wave from behind the wheel when she dropped Bella off or picked her up. She didn't strike Erin as a very happy person.

Erin had been out on her own when she was eighteen. So had Vic. There was no reason Bella had to leave home when she was eighteen. Her part-time salary certainly wasn't enough to support her. Erin couldn't afford to give her more hours and pay her more, so she was glad that Bella wasn't too independent. She didn't want to lose Bella, but she wondered if Bella would be happier if she took a bit more initiative and stood up for herself.

"Family style for dinner?" Terry asked.

"Yeah, that sounds good."

COUP DE GLACE

Terry turned his head to look over at her. "You sound very far away."

Erin forced herself to look at Terry and smile, bringing her attention back to him. "Sorry. Just tired at the end of the week, I guess."

"Maybe Bella needs to take a few more hours on so you can cut back a little."

"Mmm. Maybe. Vic would agree with you."

"Where is Vic today? Did she and Willie have a good time?"

"I don't know. Haven't heard from them yet."

He looked at her, raising his eyebrows. "Oho? Is that so?"

"They didn't come back last night. Unless they went to Willie's. They didn't end up at Vic's."

"Well. That's a step forward in their relationship."

Erin nodded. "Hopefully, that means everything went well. He's stayed over before when bad things have happened... when she was being harassed. I just hope it wasn't anything like that."

"Not likely. Away from home, no one would know anything was different about her. She looks just like any other girl."

They pulled into the family restaurant and seated themselves on arrival. After ordering, Erin tried to relax and decompress from her day.

"What do you know about Bella's family?" she asked Terry. "She's never mentioned her dad and I've never asked."

"There's never been a man in the picture. It's just been Bella and her mom. Her mom had been away, but she moved back here before Bella was born. I don't know if her father was someone here in town or from somewhere else. I've never heard any explanation."

"Poor kid. It's tough being raised without a dad."

Terry shrugged. "These days, lots of kids are."

"If it's just the two of them all alone on the farm, I guess that's why her mom is so protective."

Terry nodded his agreement and had a sip of water.

"And probably why Bella is scared of her own shadow," Erin added. "I mean, not literally of her own shadow, but she's certainly got a thing about ghosts."

"Haints," Terry said with a teasing smile.

"Haints?"

"That's the local word for ghosts. Learn the lingo."

"I haven't heard that before. Well, maybe a couple of times, but I didn't know what it meant."

"Haints. Haunts. What haunts a haunted house."

"Oh, I see." Erin smiled and shook her head. "I don't remember Clementine ever using that one. But then, I haven't exactly been around for a long time."

"Bella is afraid of haints?"

"Mortally. Scared as a... I don't know. What's really scared?"

"A long-tailed cat in a room full of rockers?"

"I think that's jumpy, but it will have to do. She is really terrified of gho-haints. I don't think I can say that without cracking up! She's afraid to go downstairs to use the loo. She has to run down the street, where she doesn't have to go down to the basement. She's sure that my basement is haunted because that's where Angela died."

"But since we solved her murder and sent the culprit to prison, doesn't that mean she would be at rest now? Why would she be haunting you now?"

"Don't ask me. I don't know how it works."

Terry chuckled.

"She asked me to look into her grandmother's death years ago," Erin told him.

"Why would you do that? You told her no, right?"

Uh-huh," Erin nodded. "I told her I'm no detective."

"Her grandmother's death?" Terry stared off into space as if trying to remember what had happened.

COUP DE GLACE

The waitress brought them their plates, and Terry and Erin ate in silence for a few minutes.

"I only have a vague recollection," Terry said. "I wasn't with the police department back then. I was just a kid, but I remember there being talk about something happening to her grandmother." He shook his head. "I'll have to look it up. Why does Bella want you to look into it?"

"Because I gather her grandmother haunts the barn. So Bella can't go in there. She'd like to be able to go in there without being scared."

"Oh." Terry shoveled mashed potatoes into his mouth. "Okay, then."

"Like I said. She's scared of… haints. Really scared."

When Erin got back, she saw Willie's truck in front of the house and breathed a sigh of relief. Not because she'd been worried anything had happened to Vic. Not really. But she couldn't help being a little concerned when Vic didn't return when she was expected to. Erin was like a mother with grown children who still worried about them, just a little, and wondered where they were and what they were doing.

Erin parked her own car and went into the house, not sure whether Vic would be there or in her own apartment in back. She smiled when she heard Vic's voice addressing Orange Blossom.

"There she is, Blossom. There's your mommy, home again."

Marshmallow, the toasted-brown and white rabbit, hopped up to Erin before Orange Blossom got there, so he got the first scratches and pats.

"Hello, you soft, fluffy, beautiful bun!" She scratched behind his ears and let the rabbit snuffle her toes, investigating all the smells she brought home with her.

The cat sat on his haunches a few feet away, looking tall and regal and completely unconcerned with the attention his fellow was getting. Erin knew it was all an act. They had a strong rivalry going. Erin kept an eye on the cat while patting Marshmallow and giving him attention, until the rabbit decided he'd had enough for the moment and hopped away. Erin looked at Orange Blossom.

"I know. You aren't looking for any attention, are you? You just live here. You're a cat, not a lap dog."

Blossom gave her a long, slow blink. Erin stepped over to him and picked him up, pulling him to her chest and cuddling him. Orange Blossom immediately began to purr, loud and satisfied.

"Now are you going to talk to me?" Erin asked, not used to his being so quiet. He was always so chatty. The silent treatment was something new. Maybe it was a sign he was growing up and wasn't a needy kitten or adolescent anymore.

Orange Blossom chirruped in response. Erin talked nonsense with him for a few minutes, scratching his ears and chin. Vic stood in the doorway and watched them, her eyes sparkling.

"You ended up being longer than you expected?" Erin asked.

"Yes. A little," Vic agreed. She smiled.

"Are you going to tell me all about it?"

Vic considered, then shook her head. "Not all about it, no. Just… that we had a really nice time. It was a great break, I feel like I had a week-long vacation. I'm so relaxed. How did everything go here? Any trouble at the bakery?"

"No, everything went smoothly. Bella was there, and we didn't have any unexpected problems. Had dinner with Terry." Erin shrugged. "And now you're home safe and sound, so I'm happy."

"Good. Cuppa tea before bed?"

"That sounds good."

Erin followed Vic into the kitchen, the animals trailing them to get their treats. Erin put out some bread and jam while Vic put the kettle on and looked through the supply of teas to pick something out.

"I don't know if we're ever going to get through all of Clementine's teas," Vic said. "She must have put up a ten-year supply!"

"All the leftover inventory from when she shut down the tea shop. I don't think it will take ten years, but maybe a couple more, anyway."

While they waited for the kettle to boil, Vic got a stick of celery out for Marshmallow and Erin flicked a couple of kitty treats across the floor for Orange Blossom to chase. Vic giggled when the cat nearly skidded straight into the cupboards after galloping after one. Marshmallow kept one eye on Orange Blossom as he nibbled sedately on his celery.

They sat down at the table and Erin breathed in the lemon balm scent carried by the steam. Vic looked over the jars of Jam Lady jam and picked out the blackberry. Erin snagged the strawberry.

Vic shook her head. "I can't believe you can still eat strawberry jam after getting poisoned."

Erin looked down at it. "It's really good."

"You're not afraid that Mr. Jam Lady put poison in another one?"

"No." Erin didn't point out that if Roger had poisoned another jar of jam, it didn't have to be the strawberry. It could just as easily have been the blackberry that Vic had chosen.

"I guess this will be the last of the Jam Lady jam," Vic sighed.

Erin spread jam on her bread. "Unless Mary Lou or the boys take over. Or if Roger gets out."

Vic looked at Erin over the rim of her teacup. "They wouldn't let him go, would they?"

"I don't think so. Even if they decide he wasn't responsible because of his brain damage… they still can't just let him go free, because of the danger he could hurt someone else."

Vic nodded her agreement. "I feel bad for Mary Lou."

"Yeah. Things are going to be tough for them."

Erin smothered a yawn. "Sorry. I slept in, I shouldn't be tired."

"You work hard. Of course you're tired. You can head to bed as soon as we're done. Sooner, if you want."

"I'll want to read for a few minutes. Write a few things down."

"Read...? Oh, Clementine's journal? Come across anything interesting?" Vic was always careful not to ask anything too intrusive. She didn't ask specifics, like whether Clementine knew what had happened to Erin's parents or had said anything about the possibility of taking care of eight-year-old Erin.

Erin nodded. "She mentioned a missing woman. Strange, because I never saw anything in the local papers about it. And it's not like I would have missed it. I was looking for information about a missing man, I would definitely have noticed a missing woman."

"Maybe she was found again before the weekly was published. Or maybe it wasn't widely known. Just because Clementine knew about it, that doesn't mean the local media would have gotten ahold of it. We don't know."

"True," Erin agreed tentatively.

"Or they might have decided it was unsubstantiated gossip and they couldn't print it. Who was it?"

"I'd have to check the names again. Proust? I don't remember their first names."

Vic raised her eyebrows. "Proust? Or Prost?"

It wasn't until then that Erin made the connection. "Prost? You mean Bella?"

Vic nodded. "That is Bella's last name, isn't it?"

The pieces started to click together. "Oh, no..."

"What?"

COUP DE GLACE

"Bella asked me if I would look into her grandmother's death, a cold case. I told her no, I'm not a private investigator… and then Clementine's journal… I never made the connection. This missing woman must have been her grandmother."

Chapter Four

ERIN DIDN'T NORMALLY HAVE Bella in on a Monday, unless it was to take the afternoon shift when she or Vic had a doctor's appointment or another errand that couldn't be put off. She didn't quite know what to say to Bella. She dithered around until it was late enough in the morning to make calls without waking people up, and then tried Bella's number. The number Erin had was, luckily, Bella's cell phone, so she wouldn't be waking the whole family by ringing the landline. Though 'the whole family' only meant Bella's mother. It wasn't like there would be sleeping children.

"Hello? Erin? Is everything okay? Didn't Vic get back? You should have called me last night."

"No, everything is fine. Vic did get back, and she's working today; we don't need you to cover an emergency shift."

"Oh. Okay… so what did you need me for, then? I put in my timesheet. I left it in your basket."

"Yes, I saw. It looks fine. I'm just… I'm having a staff meeting at the end of the day today, and I wondered if you would like to join in. Help us to make some decisions."

"Really?" Bella's voice perked up. "That would be awesome! I'd love to hear what you guys talk about, even if I didn't have any say in what the decision would be."

Erin felt a little bit guilty about that. There weren't a lot of decisions to be made at the staff meeting, but she'd have to be sure to ask Bella's opinion on a few things, just to get her involved. She probably should have been having staff meetings with both Vic and Bella for some months already, but it had never occurred to her to make it official and to invite Bella along.

"Great!" Erin said. "I'll see you here at about five, if that's okay?"

"I'll be there!"

Normally they were still open at five, but Erin could turn the sign over early. With Bella to help with the clean-up, Erin would be able to have the staff meeting and still not be home too late.

Bella's mother dropped her off just before five.

"Uh... mom wants to know how long this is going to be," Bella said, flushing pink. "What should I tell her? So she knows when to pick me up."

"It shouldn't be too long... maybe an hour? I guess that's kind of inconvenient, if she went home, she'd just have to turn around to get you again."

"It's okay," Bella assured her. "She can run some errands while she's waiting. That's not bad."

"Maybe we should drive you home after. Would that be better?"

"No, really. It's okay. Mom will pick me up. I just have to tell her when." Bella ducked back out and leaned down to talk to her mother in the car.

"Maybe this was a bad idea," Erin said to Vic.

"It's fine. Don't be so worried. It's about time we had a formal staff meeting."

In a few minutes, they had finished cleaning up. There wasn't a boardroom or any place suited for a business meeting, but they made do, using their stools at the kitchen counters.

"We've got a few things going on," Erin said. "I'm expecting the delivery of the new freezer sometime in the next week. Not sure what day it will actually show up here."

The residents of Bald Eagle Falls were used to how unreliable delivery service could be. No one wanted to make a special trip to Bald Eagle Falls, and it took too long for several deliveries to collect to make it worthwhile.

"Why do we need a new freezer?" Bella asked, throwing a glance toward the stairs to the basement, where the storage freezers were located. "I thought the old ones were working just fine."

"Not like those ones," Erin explained. "It's a display freezer with a glass front, so we can sell frozen goods and have them on display. Cakes, popsicles, frozen lemonade, whatever we want."

"Oh, great idea, with summer coming," Bella enthused. "Homemade ice cream would be amazing."

Erin nodded. She hadn't grown up in Bald Eagle Falls, and found the heat oppressive, but she thought that even the born-and-bred Tennesseans would appreciate the option of frozen treats in the summer. And it would allow her to freeze day-old goods and not have to waste as much. She was looking forward to the arrival of the freezer with more excitement than was natural.

They went on to other items on the agenda and were done in half an hour. Erin pretended to be studying her list of prioritized items.

"Bella, you were talking about your grandma and grandpa the other day. But I forget what you said their names were."

Bella frowned and tilted her head, not understanding why Erin would bring it up. "Uh… give me a minute… usually, it's just 'grandma and grandpa,' you know? Uh… Ezekiel and Martha, I think. I really should know their names better, they're the only grandparents I'll ever have. Why?"

"Well…" Erin considered lying about it. But she couldn't think of anything that would explain why she was looking for the names of her employee's grandparents.

COUP DE GLACE

"You were asking me about looking into your grandma's death the other day, so I was curious about what exactly happened…"

Bella's eyes squinted slightly at Erin, frowning. "I don't really know much. My mom doesn't like to talk about it. I guess… nobody really knows what happened to her. People say maybe my grandpa had something to do with it, but why would he do that? They were old! They'd been married to each other forever. Men don't just suddenly kill their wives for no reason when they're that old."

Erin and Vic exchanged glances. "Well, we can't know anyone's motives without looking into it," Erin said. "Just because he was old, that doesn't mean he wasn't capable of doing something to hurt her. People still get jealous… greedy… or they have something wrong with their brains…"

"You think he was crazy? I don't think my grandpa was crazy."

"No, I don't know anything about it," Erin said. "I'm just saying… we never can be sure of what motives a person might have, without knowing everything about their past. Even knowing, sometimes we would never guess…" Erin thought about the murders that she had had an intimate peek at during her short stay in Bald Eagle Falls. Fear, jealousy, greed, an instant of anger… so many senseless deaths.

Bella pulled a lock of hair into her mouth and chewed on it. "Does that mean you changed your mind about looking into it? Will you see if you can solve what happened to her?"

"I don't know," Erin was honest. "I still don't want to be a detective. I'm just a baker. A full-time baker. But I admit I am curious…" she trailed off. "My Aunt Clementine wrote about it in her journal and I was just reading what she wrote. I don't know whether there is any real insight in Clementine's observations, but at least it is a first-hand account. Someone who was actually around when it happened, instead of it being a fuzzy memory from a long time ago.

"It's in your Auntie Clem's journal?"

Erin nodded. "I haven't read it all... but she's mentioned it once or twice so far."

"That's so cool! It's almost like we're related!"

"Mary Lou says everyone on the mountain is related. Everyone who's been here for any length of time, anyway. She says we're all kin."

"Will you at least let me know what it says? I'd really like to hear from someone who knew them."

Erin nodded in agreement. "Sure. I'll let you know what I find out."

Mrs. Sturm finally got poor old Ezekiel to let her in, and there is no sign of Martha anywhere. At least there is no moldering body in the living room or the bed, but that doesn't explain what has happened to her. Ezekiel said she's just off visiting, but Martha doesn't drive, and no one has driven her anywhere. At least not that anyone I have talked to knows about. Someone would have seen her if she'd taken the bus. Could Ezekiel have dropped her off somewhere? He can't explain where she has gone, other than general statements that she is off visiting, and it is no one's business where and the rest of the details. He is entitled to his own privacy, and yet...

Ezekiel still denies the sheriff access to his property. I asked the sheriff why he can't just go and take a look around, see if there are any new graves or disturbed areas, but apparently even for that, he needs permission. Mrs. Sturm only looked around the house, she didn't get a chance to look around the rest of the property.

It remains a mystery.

Erin handed the journal silently to Vic, who took it from her without a word. Vic looked at Erin's face, then dropped her eyes to the paper. Erin watched her eyes go back and forth as she read the passage. Then she shook her head and handed it back.

"So they really do think that it was her grandfather? Not a stranger from out of town? An old man?"

"Being old doesn't stop anyone from making mistakes."

"But there's no evidence. None in there, anyway. If we are going to take the case, we'll have to talk to the people who knew them."

"But they'll just remember that they thought he was guilty, don't you think? Besides, we are not taking on the case. I'm just… looking."

Vic raised her eyebrows. "Sure. Just looking."

Chapter Five

ERIN HAD NO PREMONITION when she got up in the morning that anything was going to happen. It was a bright, clear spring day, no 'dark and stormy night.' No spooky music. Everything about her day suggested that it was just going to be a normal, routine day like any other. Even her reading of Clementine's journal the night before didn't keep her from getting a good night's sleep and starting off bright-eyed and bushy-tailed the next morning.

She and Vic went to the bakery as usual, and everything proceeded normally.

Until the afternoon lull, when the bells jingling announced a new customer, and Erin looked up to see a tall, mysterious stranger.

It wasn't a strange man, it was a woman, her red hair in cornrows draped over her cheeks and shoulders, not gathered under the colorful scarf wound around her head. Her makeup was dramatic, eyelids smoky and lips red, and she had large gold hoop earrings. Her peasant dress was a shimmery blue. Her nails were red, and her hands adorned with numerous heavy, old-looking rings.

And she wasn't a stranger. because once Erin took a good look at her, she could see that it was the face of someone familiar.

"Well, there she is," Reg Rawlins said. "How's my favorite sister?"

"How can she be your sister?" Vic demanded. "I thought your only sister was Charley, and she's just a half-sister. Who is this Regina person?"

It was understandable that Vic was protective. Erin had taken care of Vic when she was in need. Vic had shot a man who had been trying to kill Erin. Erin was always ready to step in whenever Vic was being harassed. They took care of each other, lived and worked together, and were closer than sisters. Closer than Erin and Charley, anyway.

Erin glanced toward the door that led back out to the front customer area, trying to ensure that Reg couldn't see or hear them.

"She *was* my sister," she said. "A foster sister. But it's been a long time since we were anything to each other. Everyone goes their own way, and foster kids don't get the option of staying in touch."

"How did she know where to find you? And why? What's she doing here?"

"I don't know, since she only just got here, and I excused myself to talk to you."

"It can't be good."

"Well, it could be," Erin suggested. "Maybe she just came to let me know… how she's doing in life. That she's okay. Maybe she's getting in contact with everyone from her old life…"

"What are the odds of that?"

"Well… rare enough that I've never heard of it happening before."

"Yeah, that's what I thought."

Erin didn't tell Vic that Reg had been in contact with her before, after they were both out of the foster care system. And Reg hadn't just been looking for old friends to reconnect with. Erin wasn't happy to see her again.

Vic took a deep breath in, then breathed it out slowly. "She's here. So I guess you need to at least say hi to her. Give her a chance to say what it is that she wants." Vic wasn't going to be fooled into thinking that Reg just wanted to see her old family members again.

Erin nodded and took Vic out to the front of the shop.

"Hey, Reg, I wanted you to meet my friend, and my assistant in the bakery, Vic Webster. Vic... this is Reg Rawlins." Erin paused. "Are you going by Rawlins?"

"It's as good a name as any for now. What's in a name?"

Erin looked away from Reg, not wanting to be hypnotized by her new look. "It's good to see you again," she said automatically. "It's been a long time."

"Yeah. Well, it wasn't easy to find you, sis. Surprise, surprise, you're using your real name again. I didn't expect to find you under Erin Price."

Erin could feel Vic's eyes on her, interested and hoping for an explanation. But Vic wasn't exactly using her birth name either. She knew there were plenty of reasons for starting fresh, where no one knew you or your past.

Erin gave a shrug. "What's in a name?" she echoed.

Reg laughed. She looked at Vic. "Has she told you all about the mischief we caused in foster care?"

Vic smiled. "No, I haven't heard about this."

"It's nothing, Vic," Erin said quickly. "Kids do stuff. I tried hard to be good, so that foster families wouldn't send me away. I wanted to just stay in one place, with one family."

"Sure," there was a hint of a sneer in Reg's tone. "You wanted to stay with a family, runaway Erin? You had a funny way of showing it."

Erin shrugged again. "Kids do stuff."

Reg nodded, looking over the treats in the display case. "They sure do. And you were a runner. Caused foster moms no end of trouble. What's good here?"

"Everything is good," Erin said briskly. "It's all made from scratch. All gluten-free and nut-free. There are options if you are vegan or are allergic to one of the other major allergens; I try to make sure everyone can eat something."

COUP DE GLACE

Erin thought of Bertie Braceling and experienced a pang. She had thought she'd have years to try to develop a line of treats that were good for him. But like Carolyn, he was gone. It was too late to help him now.

"I don't have any allergies," Reg said. "How about... chocolate zucchini muffin?"

"Good choice," Vic approved, helping to take some of the weight of the conversation away from Erin. "They are always so moist and flavorful." She used the tongs to put one into a package for Reg.

Erin didn't bother to ring it up. "First one is free."

Reg slid the muffin partway out of the wrapper and took a large bite. "Oh, yeah. That's good stuff! This is gluten free? It tastes pretty good!"

"That's the idea," Erin agreed coolly.

Reg munched on the muffin, analyzing Erin. "No need to order fireworks and a big brass band. But you could show a little more excitement over seeing your long-lost sister."

"I found out recently that I actually do have a biological sister I never knew about," Erin said. "I was really nervous about meeting her. But it has been a while since I saw you last. Are you... just passing through?"

"Not exactly. I was hoping you could put me up for a few days and we could talk old times."

"Reg..." Erin glanced over at Vic, wishing that she'd leave them to have a private conversation. "I really don't have the time for old times. I have a new life now. I don't want to screw it up."

"I'm not doing anything to get you into trouble. What's wrong with reconnecting with an old friend? You and I *were* friends. We used to do things together. Even after we were both out of foster care."

"I know... I'm not trying to be stuck up... I just... stuff from the past... things didn't work out so well in the past and I don't want to repeat the same mistakes. You like to... stir things up."

Vic gave a little snicker. "I think I've heard the same said about someone else around here a time or two."

Erin glared at her. "Not helping, Vic."

"Sorry." Vic held her hands up. "Ignore me. I'm not even here. In fact, I'll go in back and wash some dishes. Just give me a shout if you need a hand with customers."

Vic retreated into the kitchen. Erin turned back to Reg.

"So how about it?" Reg asked. "Can we do supper?"

Erin was reluctant to close the bakery at the end of the day, knowing that once she was finished, she was going to be meeting Reg at the Chinese restaurant for supper. Her stomach was tied in knots and her head whirled with memories of her and Reg in foster care and later as young women out on their own, and the crazy stuff they'd been involved in. Reg was always the leader, and it seemed like Erin was always game to join in whatever nutty scheme Reg had devised. Some of them had been innocent games where no one was harmed. Others...

"She seems nice," Vic said.

Erin was jarred from her memories. "What?"

"Your foster sister, Reg. She seems like she's nice. The two of you must have had a lot of fun together."

"Uh... yeah. Of course. It was nice having her in the picture, back then. I needed someone who... liked me and wanted to do things with me."

Vic nodded as she scrubbed the cooling racks. "Her makeup and everything was very dramatic. Does she always look like that? Like a fortune teller looking for a place to happen?"

Erin hesitated. "She's had... a lot of different looks over the years. I don't know what this one is about yet. I guess she'll tell me at dinner."

"You'll have a nice time," Vic said firmly. Erin was obviously radiating her anxiety about the meal. Vic could read it in her face and body language just as clearly as if she'd been announcing it out loud.

"I'll try. I'm sure it will be nice… it's just… it's been a long time, and things have changed a lot since we saw each other last."

"Sure. You've grown up. A lot of things change between when you're a kid and when you're an independent adult," Vic agreed with authority.

Erin looked at her. Vic was *barely* a legal adult. Erin had been older than she was when she'd seen Reg last.

Vic grinned and got a little pink. "Just because I'm young, that doesn't mean it's not true."

"I suppose not. I'm just… I've got a bad feeling about this. Reg Rawlins is trouble."

"You can always tell her no. She can't just roll into town and expect you to take her in. Southern hospitality only goes so far."

Erin put mixing bowls away in the cupboard. "I can't even figure out what she's doing in Tennessee. She's never been this far south in her life. She can't have come this far just to see me."

"All the way from…?"

"Uh…" Erin thought back, trying to place the memories of Reg in a concrete time and place. "Massachusetts, I think. Yeah… pretty sure…"

"It is a long way," Vic admitted. "Who knows, maybe she is on her way to see someone else. Just a few days in Tennessee… we could handle that. You do have a guest room."

"Once she gets in…"

"You make her sound like a disease. Is she really that bad?"

"No. She was a good friend… we helped each other out… I just don't know what to think."

"Wait and see what she has to say. Then you can decide."

Chapter Six

MADDIE BURNS, ONE OF the hostesses at the Chinese restaurant, greeted Erin and gave her a look of puzzlement as she looked for Terry or Vic, and found Erin to be alone.

"I'm supposed to be meeting an out-of-town friend here," Erin explained. "Anyone unfamiliar here?"

"Oh, the gypsy." Maddie turned and pointed Reg out. "Right over there. Do you want a menu?"

"No, I don't need one. Thanks."

Erin went to Reg's table. 'Gypsy' was a good description of Reg. She didn't have the bone structure of a Roma gypsy, but she looked like a gypsy straight out of a children's fairy tale with her colorful headscarf, dramatic makeup, and loose skirt. Erin sat down across from her. She looked her old friend over one more time.

"Okay... tell me what this is about."

"What? I came to see you. To connect with you again. Why are you acting like there's something wrong with that?"

"You're all dressed up for some scam. So tell me. What's it all about?"

Reg tilted her head to the side, considering her answer. She ran her fingers through her narrow braids and rubbed the back of her head. "Just looking to make a little green."

"This is just a little town. You can't make anything here."

"I can't make anything here?" Reg snorted. "The looks I'm getting... people are falling all over themselves to get a good look at the stranger in town. Once they hear that I'm a medium, they won't stop knocking at my door."

"A medium?" Erin rubbed her face, tired after the long day and not wanting to hear about Reg's newest scheme.

"You know I've always had a talent for figuring people out," Reg said evenly. "I've always had a special intuition about things…"

"And that makes you a medium? Like a psychic?"

"So much more than just a psychic," Reg protested. "That doesn't even begin to describe my range of talents. Psychic readings are just one of the many spiritual gifts that I have. Healing, communing with the dead, palm and card reading, tea leaves…"

"You think people will fall for that?"

"What do you mean 'fall for' it? It's the truth. It doesn't matter whether people believe it or not. That's up to them."

"You want people to pay you for looking at their hands and making up some nonsense about what is going to happen to them in the future."

"Nonsense? No. I want to help people to realize their full potential. I am more like a life coach. Not some… charlatan who is just trying to bilk people out of their hard-earned money."

"You're not a psychic."

"I didn't say I was. I said that I am sensitive to impressions about people. I can help them to become who they are really destined to be. To find their true path to happiness."

"And how are you going to do this?"

"Talking with them. Picking up clues in their speech and manner. Reading them. You can tell a lot about a person just by looking at them. Add in some visiting to find out who they are and where they are going in life, and I can give you an accurate reading of just about anyone in the world. You don't think I can?"

"That, I can believe," Erin agreed. "But why do you have to surround that with this…" Erin flipped her hand to indicate Reg's costume, "this mysticism?"

"Because people like it. They're impressed by it. It signals to them that I'm serious about what I do, and they can trust me. If you meet people's expectations, they will take you for a professional. This is just me… meeting people's expectations."

"And you're going to tell them that what you're doing is just a cold reading?"

"I'll tell them what they want to hear. If they want me to couch it in spiritual terms instead of straightforward like you do, then that's how I'll explain it. Why would you have a problem with that?"

Maddie Burns brought over the dishes that Reg had ordered while she'd been waiting for Erin to arrive. Both women helped themselves to a sampling from the platters.

"My problem is that it's nonsense," Erin said. "There's nothing spiritual about it. There's nothing mystical. You're just someone trying to make a buck off of being observant."

Reg *tsked*, shaking her head. "Okay. You don't believe in God, right?"

Erin nodded. "That's right. I am an atheist. I don't believe in any of these secret powers you claim to have. Or that anyone else claims to have. I don't believe in prophecy or revelation or any of the things that happened in the ancient texts. Stories are stories. They change over time. Their purpose changes over time. But they are still just that—stories."

"And you go around telling that to everyone you meet."

Erin pressed her lips together. "No. I don't tell that to anyone."

"You just keep it to yourself and let them believe and practice what they like."

Erin nodded. "Yes. Exactly."

"Then why would you expect me to do anything different? I just frame the experience in the terms they are familiar with. I'm not lying to them. I'm just meeting them at their own level."

Erin shook her head. She ate a few bites of her dinner. "Whatever it is you're doing, don't expect me to help you with it."

Reg didn't say anything.

For a few minutes, they just ate, making routine comments about the food and what they liked. Just as if they were two friends who had met for dinner because they enjoyed each other's company.

"I need somewhere to stay until I can get myself established," Reg said finally, as they were both getting full and slowing down. "Not for long. I'm sure I can find a little rental somewhere that I can afford."

Erin had already told her no. She clenched her teeth in irritation but did her best to keep her expression calm and pleasant. "You can't just drop in on people and expect them to put you up."

"Not just anyone," Reg agreed. "But when it's your sister? Your best friend?"

"We haven't been sisters for a long time."

"Come on, Erin. The number of times I pulled your butt out of the fire? Erin and Reg Rawlins against the world. You don't remember?"

The trouble was, Erin did remember. Every time Reg had rescued her, it was Reg who had gotten her in trouble in the first place. It had been the two of them against the world, when maybe they should have been trying to get along in the world instead of fighting it every step of the way. Reg had encouraged Erin to fight her foster parents, social workers, school teachers, and anyone else in authority over her. She had encouraged Erin's natural propensity to rebel if someone told her she had to do something. She'd thought it funny when Erin ran.

Mrs. Bloom, her social worker, had seen the dynamic between them and had tried more than once to convince Erin that Reg was bad for her, which only served to push Erin closer to her. When she had eventually found other homes for the two of them, splitting them up, the decision had caused an irreparable rift between Erin and her social worker. Erin would never again trust Mrs. Bloom or anyone else at social services with any information about her life.

"What are you thinking about?" Reg prodded, her voice soft.

"Mrs. Bloom."

"The dragon! Man, she was terrible, wasn't she? She had it out for me right from the start."

"Yeah, she did," Erin agreed. "She saw right through you."

That gave Reg pause. She considered Erin's words. "Are you saying she was right about me?"

Erin raised her brows. "She *was*."

Reg laughed it off. "I suppose you're right. But you needed someone on your side, Erin. You had to learn how to stand up for yourself."

"I stood up for myself."

"I mean using words, not just being stubborn or running away. Actually telling people what you thought."

Erin chewed on the last piece of noodle on her plate, considering. "Well, now I'm telling you. I'm not putting you up."

"But you are," Reg insisted, mischievous eyes sparkling.

"No, I'm not. Why would I?"

"Because I'm your sister, and that's stronger than your personal preference. Maybe you don't want to put me up, but because I'm your sister, you will anyway."

"It's a long time since we were sisters."

"Sisters forever. That's what you promised. That's what we promised each other. Not just sisters until we went to different families. Sisters forever."

COUP DE GLACE

Promises of devotion. Fierce hugs. Lots of tears. Erin could see the two of them together in her mind's eye. *Sisters forever. No matter what.*

The world could end, and they would still be sisters. No matter what any parent or social worker did, they would always be sisters.

Maddie Burns brought their bill, together with two factory-produced fortune cookies on a little plate. Erin unwrapped one of the fortune cookies and broke it open.

Be prepared for the unexpected.

Erin rolled her eyes and dropped the slip of paper onto the table. How could anyone prepare for what wasn't expected?

"I thought you didn't believe in fortune telling," Reg said.

"I don't."

"Then why did you open your cookie?"

Erin's face warmed. "I just wanted to see what it said. That doesn't mean I believe it. Just that it's interesting to see what they come up with."

"Sure. And because deep down inside, part of you wants to believe that it's true. Part of you wants to believe that you can catch just a glimpse of your future by reading a fortune cookie. The little girl part of you still wants to believe that the fortune inside is true, and that it will bring you something good."

When Erin had been little, she had not been a non-believer. She had hoped that there really was something to religion, mysticism, and magic. She wished on stars and birthday candles. She crossed her fingers, jumped over sidewalk cracks, and knelt by her bed to pray in the homes where she was told to. But there hadn't been any breaks. None of her prayers or wishes came true. By the time she turned eighteen, she was a firm non-believer against anything supernatural or unworldly. By then, she knew that it was all nonsense, no matter how many people believed.

They were just holding on to something for comfort. Like a child dragging her teddy bear from one home to the next, thinking it would keep her safe in the night. But it never did.

"A few days," Erin finally said. "No more than a week. You start looking for a place of your own now, this minute. You can't stay with me forever."

"Never intended to," Reg agreed. "I just need to crash on your couch for a day or two while I get on my feet."

"Not the couch. I have a guest room. And you're there as a guest, so act like one. Not like you own the place or have some right to be there. You're there because I'm a nice person, not because I owe you anything."

Reg nodded. "Sure. Of course. And I'm sorry to be crashing on you like this. I didn't plan it that way."

Erin wasn't sure she wanted to know exactly what Reg had been planning.

Chapter Seven

REG GOT HER MEAGER belongings settled and decided on a hot bath, so she was out of the way for a while. Erin breathed a sigh of relief. When Vic came into the house, her head turned toward the sound of the water running in the bathroom immediately. "I thought you weren't going to…?"

"She talked me into it," Erin sighed. "Just pretend she's not here. That's what I'm doing."

"How long?"

"Just a few days."

Vic shook her head. "Always taking in strays, aren't you?"

"I didn't want to. She's not a house cat, she's a tiger kitten. Sooner or later, it's going to turn out badly."

"I hope not."

Erin shrugged. "That's just the way it is with Reg. It always ends with disaster."

Vic stooped to pick up Orange Blossom, another member of the family who was not happy about a newcomer in the house. He bumped his head against Vic's chin, demanding attention. Vic's eyes were troubled.

"It will be okay," Erin reassured her. "It won't work out how Reg has planned, but… mostly that will be bad for her, not us. She'll get over it."

"Oh, it's not that. I get it. Some people just bring drama with them everywhere they go. I gather your sister is one of those people."

"Lots of drama," Erin agreed.

"Yeah. I wasn't thinking about her. I was thinking about Willie."

Erin was startled by the change in subject. She sat down on the couch and drew up her feet under her. "Willie? What about him? Everything is... okay, isn't it?"

Vic hadn't had much to say about her overnight stay with Willie. Erin hoped that the two of them had gotten along all right and hadn't run into any irreconcilable differences.

"Everything is great. We're working through things. Taking our time. Sharing what we feel comfortable with. Really good."

Erin nodded. She sensed a 'but' in there somewhere.

"He's looking for a new job."

"Oh," Erin nodded. "That's great."

In all the time she had known Willie, and from what she understood about his past, for a long time all Willie had done were odd jobs. He had his mines, and Erin didn't know what sort of metals he got out of them or how he refined them. That didn't take all of his time or provide the living he needed to take care of his own needs or Vic's. So he always had other things going on. Courier deliveries, flyer distribution, helping the seniors with their yard work. He was one of the busiest people Erin knew.

"I don't think it's great," Vic objected. "Why does he need to change his path now, just because we're together? He should still be able to do what he wants."

"Well, no one is stopping him from finding things he likes."

"I feel like I am." Vic sat down on one of the recliners, still holding Orange Blossom.

"What do you mean? You haven't told him where he can or can't work, have you?"

COUP DE GLACE

"No. But he's gotten into his head that he has to have a steady, stable job. Nine to five, five days a week. Like a 'normal' person."

Erin was horrified. It didn't sound like a bad idea on the surface but, knowing Willie as she did, she knew he would be miserable in a job like that. He liked the ability to be flexible, to decide how much work he wanted and when he would complete it. While these odd jobs often took him out of town for a day or two, he found ways to be with Vic the rest of the week, and the varied jobs kept him happy and productive. She had no idea how he would manage the stresses of a routine office job. He'd be bored. He'd be overwhelmed. He wouldn't know what to do with himself. Maybe it would still allow him enough time to do his mining; his weekends would be free, at least.

"Why is he doing that?"

"I don't know." Vic's voice was anguished. "I've told him he doesn't need to do it. That I don't think he'll be happy with a job like that, but he's sure it's the only way to go. He says if he's going to be a family man, he needs to have something stable."

Erin raised her brows. "A family man?"

"We were talking, when we went into the city. About what we wanted, where we wanted to go with our lives. I said that I wanted a family, and he thought he did too. We were both happy with that. I was glad to hear that he was interested in the same things as I was. But then when we got back here, and he decided he was going to get a full-time office job…" Vic shook her head, eyes shiny with tears.

"An office job? He's not even going to find something that is outside…?"

"That's the plan. White collar worker. That's what he thinks I want or expect from him, what a family man should do."

"There are plenty of family men who don't have white collar office jobs. That's just silly. Didn't you tell him…?"

"Don't you think I tried to tell him that I wasn't expecting him to change what he was and didn't want him to give up his... his way of life? Of course I did. I've told him every which way to Sunday. But he thinks it's just words, that I'm just being nice. He's sure that I really want him to be... normal."

"Do you want me to try to explain it to him?"

"I don't know. I don't know if that will make it better or worse. I can't tell him that he can do whatever he wants, and then say that he can't switch to banker's hours if he wants to. If it's what he really wants... I can't tell him not to."

Erin frowned. "I suppose. But you and I both know he's going to hate it!"

"Of course he is."

Vic stroked Orange Blossom briskly, in a way that made him yip and yowl, squirming to get comfortable.

"You both want a family?" Erin asked, changing the direction of the conversation slightly. "So... you would adopt?"

Vic nodded. "Seeing as I don't have the equipment. Or use a surrogate. Maybe we'll foster."

Erin's feelings warred. The product of the foster care system herself, she wasn't inclined to recommend it to anyone. But until someone came up with a system that worked better, there would always be foster kids in need of good parents. Vic and Willie would be good parents, given some time and experience, but the children they parented wouldn't be their own, and Erin didn't want them having to suffer the heartbreak of separation when children inevitably had to move on to new situations.

"Just... make sure it's what you really want. A lot of people think they do, but... it's not an easy job."

"Yeah." Vic's smile seemed forced. The water in the bathroom stopped running, bringing them both back to the present. "Speaking of foster care, tell me about Reg. You guys seem like you were close."

"Yes. Maybe the closest I ever was to a foster sibling. But she also... got us in a lot of trouble. She's a... not a troublemaker, exactly. But someone who agitates others..."

"And you were her favorite target."

"I guess so," Erin agreed, surprised at how quickly Vic grasped the situation. "Even after we were both adults, out of the system, she still tracks me down, shows up in my life at the most unlikely times, and gets me involved in some grand new scheme."

"What is it this time?"

Erin shook her head, not sure how to put it into words. Calling Reg a fortune-teller or medium didn't begin to describe the grandness of what she had in mind. "I don't know. That's her own business."

The bathroom door opened, and Erin felt the moist air expanding outward, dissipating into the house. The fresh smells of soap and shampoo wafted over Erin. When Reg stepped out of the bathroom, she was wearing one of the nightgowns that had been hanging in the closet in Clementine's room, which Erin had assigned to Reg. She was already making herself at home, digging herself in, making it harder to extricate her when it was time.

"Oh, you have company. Hi, there. You're... Vic, from the bakery."

Vic nodded.

"She lives over the garage," Erin advised. "Her apartment is just across the yard," she gestured.

"I didn't know you were such good friends. That's awesome."

If Reg's intuition had been as powerful as she said it was, she should have been able to discern the strong friendship between them, especially with her knowing Erin so well.

"Yeah. We're just going to visit for a few minutes, and then I'll be heading to bed. We need to start work pretty early in the morning…"

Reg didn't take the hint. Instead, she settled in, making herself comfortable in the other recliner. "So, what's been going on with you lately?" she asked Erin. "We kind of talked about what I'm up to, but you didn't say what's up with you."

Erin blinked at her. "Well… running the bakery. That takes up most of my time. I'm up really early, work until evening, and then have a short break before bed and starting all over again."

"I don't get how you ended up with the bakery. Did you buy it? Is it like… your own start-up? I know you liked to cook, but I never thought you'd have a place of your own. Pretty hard for a foster to get up capital like that."

"It was my aunt. Clementine. She left it to me in her will. It was a tea shop when she was running it, but I didn't want to run a tea shop, I wanted a gluten-free bakery. So that's what I did."

"The muffins are good." Reg patted her stomach, as if she'd just eaten one, instead of having consumed it early in the day. "If everything else measures up, I can see why it's popular. Normally, I see gluten-free, and I think 'cardboard.' But your baking is really nice."

"Thanks. I hope I can keep growing it. I notice we've started to get some out-of-town traffic lately." Erin glanced over at Vic for her input.

"You're right," Vic agreed. "Seeing more and more people from towns nearby where people have heard there are good gluten-free treats to be had in Bald Eagle Falls. If we can get more and more of those people, we don't have to rely just on the Bald Eagle Falls residents, which would be really good."

"Especially with Charley trying to reopen The Bake Shoppe," Erin agreed.

COUP DE GLACE

"Who is Charley?" Reg asked.

"My half-sister. I just found her recently. She was my mom's daughter, but not my dad's, and I never knew about her. She inherited a bakery from her dad's side, or half of it, and she wants to open it up again as soon as she can. And I guess they're doing the transmittal before too long, which means she'll be able to open it if she wants to. As long as Davis, her brother and the owner of the other half of the bakery, doesn't object." Erin glanced over at Vic. "She wants to get full ownership, but I guess she'll be fine just to have control of it. She'll get it open as soon as she can, and then we'll have competition."

"What does she need to do to get full ownership?" Reg asked, her eyes shrewd. "Buy out her brother?"

"That would do it," Erin admitted. "But what she really wants to do is to take it away from him without paying for it. She wants to prove that he had something to do with killing his brother, and he can't profit from his crime."

"Ah," Reg nodded sagely. "Makes sense."

Erin was a little surprised at Reg's interest in business matters. The Reg of the past had always been in it for fun and fast money, and things like building a business would not have interested her. But maybe she was maturing, and she was getting interested in more than just quick, easy money.

"I still think she'll do it," Vic said. "Prove that Davis was involved in Trenton's murder, I mean. She's driven."

"And what do you do besides the bakery?" Reg asked. "You can't work all the time. What do you do for your own entertainment?"

Erin had a hard time answering that one. She spent almost every second of the day at the bakery or wrapped up in running it somehow. If she wasn't baking and selling her wares, she was working on paying the bills, writing ad copy, working through marketing plans, or thinking ahead to the next party or holiday.

"Well… not a lot," she admitted. "It takes up most of my time."

"Solving murders," Vic suggested.

Erin shot her a look. "I don't solve murders," she said quickly.

"Well, not all of them, but you've got a pretty good track record so far."

"Solving murders?" Reg repeated with wide-eyed interest. "How many have you solved?"

"Uh… well, Angela Plaint; her son Trevor; her husband, Adam; and my father. Charley's boyfriend. Joelle Biggs. That's it."

"Six," Reg counted. "And how long have you lived here?"

"About a year."

"That's one every two months. That's amazing. I know full-time PI's who don't have a record like that."

"It's just been… luck. I haven't been looking to solve murder cases and haven't been paid for it. I just sort of… fall into things…"

"You get any money for it?"

"No. I was trying to stay out of prison for most of them!"

Reg laughed. "Right in the midst of things, our Erin. Man, I miss you, sister! You always did get into the most interesting scrapes."

"Not without your help."

"Come on, you would have gotten into trouble whether I was there or not, am I right? You just couldn't help yourself."

"No," Erin protested. "I was quiet and kept to myself. I wouldn't have gotten into any trouble without your help."

"Ha!" Reg looked at Vic for help. "Tell me you don't believe her. You've seen how it happens, haven't you? She just attracts trouble, like bees to honey."

"Well..." Vic screwed up her nose and tried to think of what to say. "It's not that she's trying to, though. So I don't know if it counts."

"It counts. It goes to show that she can find trouble all by herself without me at her side."

"I suppose," Vic admitted.

"You're supposed to be on my side, traitor!" Erin said with mock hurt.

There was a knock at the door and they all looked up. Erin wasn't expecting anyone else. She went to the door and peeked through the peephole, expecting to see Terry, or maybe Mary Lou. Other people just didn't stop by for a visit. Not usually. She twisted the deadbolt and opened the door to Bella, standing there looking embarrassed and much smaller than usual.

"Bella? What are you doing here?" Erin couldn't think of what would have brought Bella to the house, especially when she didn't drive.

"Sorry," Bella apologized. "I probably should have called instead of just showing up on your doorstep. It's just, my mom is visiting a friend, and I was with her, but I was getting bored and thinking about things, and I thought I'd stop by here and see..."

Erin waited for her to finish her sentence. "Yes...? See what?"

"See if you'd figured anything out yet about my grandma."

"Uh..." Erin looked at Vic and Reg. "I haven't looked into anything. I told you, I'm not a detective. I don't think I'm going to get very far looking into an old case."

"You did before. You figured out what happened with Adam Plaint."

"Well... but I had Clementine's journal to help me out there. I wouldn't have known where the boys hid the body without the journal. And I wouldn't have known about the men being switched, if it wasn't for Bertie Braceling being involved. It was just luck…"

"But you said Clementine talked about my grandma and grandpa in her journal. So you do have a starting point. Couldn't you at least… think about it? Read it over and try to imagine what had happened?"

Reg had a big grin on her face and was obviously enjoying the fix Erin was in.

"I'm not a detective," Erin repeated, giving Reg a glare. "I'm just a baker."

"Why won't anyone talk about what happened to my grandma? Doesn't anybody care? I know it happened twenty years ago, but she must have had friends. People who cared about what happened to her."

"The journal didn't say what happened to her," Erin said. "Just that she disappeared, and Clementine was concerned about your grandpa and what had happened."

"I want to know. If you can find out what happened to her, then I can stop worrying about the barn."

"The barn?" Reg asked, leaning forward. "What about the barn?"

"It's haunted," Bella said. "Maybe if we can figure out what happened to my grandma, then she'll be able to rest, and I won't have to be scared of the barn anymore."

Reg's eyes turned to Erin, eyes inquiring whether Bella was really serious. Erin gave a slight nod.

"Maybe *I* could help you," Reg offered.

"How? Erin is the one who is good at figuring this kind of stuff out."

"I'm sure she is. Did you know I'm her sister? And I'm trained to find things like this out. To see what other people can't see. I have a special talent."

"Really?" Bella's eyes were big. "How can you find things out?"

"I have a talent." Reg was wearing a nightgown rather than the headscarf she had been wearing earlier in the day,

COUP DE GLACE

and had washed all of her makeup off, so there was no way for Bella to guess about her newfound psychic abilities. "What if I could talk to your grandmother?"

"You can't," Bella said, frustrated with having to explain it all over again. "She's dead. Or disappeared. She must be dead, or she wouldn't be haunting the barn. But I don't know what happened to her or how to fix it so that she can be at peace."

"If she's there, I can talk to her," Reg promised. "You just take me to your barn and I'll talk to her. We'll figure out what happened to her and what to do next."

Bella's big eyes got bigger and rounder. "You can talk to haints?"

Erin glanced over at Vic, amused. Score one for local dialect. But Reg was still in the dark about what a haint was. She frowned and blinked.

"Ghosts," Erin told her. "She's asking if you can talk to ghosts."

Reg nodded solemnly. "Yes! Exactly. If you take me there, I will talk to her, and we'll sort this all out."

Bella looked suddenly cautious. "I can't bring anyone to the farm unless my mom says."

Reg's brows drew down. "You're not allowed to invite anyone to your house?"

"Uh…" Bella shifted nervously. "No. Not really. I can check with Mom, she might say it's okay. But you can't tell her that you're coming to talk to my Grandma, or she'll say no."

"Doesn't your mother want to find out what happened to her mother? Why would she block it?"

"Talking to ghosts is…" Bella looked around dramatically, "that's *spiritualism*," she whispered. "Mom would never agree to that. And she's never wanted to talk to me about what happened to Grandma. She clams right up. Nobody knows what happened, but I think Mom's afraid that... people would think badly of us, if word got out."

"But people know your grandma disappeared," Erin said. "My aunt knew. What do people think happened? That she just fell off the face of the earth?"

"She's always kept it real quiet. No one ever proved that she died or that there was any foul play. She just... wasn't around anymore."

"Maybe I can come out there one day when your mom isn't around," Reg suggested. "We wouldn't have to get permission and she would never know about it. That way we wouldn't be stirring things up. I could talk to your grandma and send her on her way. Then you wouldn't have to worry about being afraid of the barn."

Bella nodded her understanding. "I guess... it's just that... she's almost always home. She doesn't go out very much, and when she does, it isn't for long. I don't know when the next time is going to be."

"The opportunity will present itself," Reg promised. "You'll just have to be patient while we wait for it. It will happen. And when it does, you give me a call." Reg felt for her pockets, but then realized she was wearing Clementine's night gown. "I'll get you my number, wait here for just a minute."

She disappeared into the guest room, and returned a minute later with a business card, which she insisted Bella take. "How else are you going to call me? Keep that. Let me know when she's gone, and I'll come straight out."

Bella handled the business card as though it were hot, holding it gingerly by the edges. "I don't want my mom to see this..."

"Then memorize it and get rid of it. Just make sure you know it when the time comes."

Bella stared down at the card, nodding dubiously.

Chapter Eight

AFTER BELLA WAS HEADED back on her way, Erin said her goodbyes to Vic. Neither of them could say much in front of Reg, but they were familiar enough with each other's facial expressions and body language to communicate the basics. Erin didn't like Reg having anything to do with Bella. Vic wasn't sure what she felt about Reg herself, but she was willing to give Reg a chance and see how things turned out. They would talk about it at the bakery in the morning, where they could do it without being overheard.

"Nice to meet you," Vic told Reg, giving her a social hug where they barely touched each other. "I guess I'll see you around."

"Maybe we'll come see you at your house next time," Reg offered. "Save you the long trip."

Vic gave a little laugh, but her eyes when she looked at Erin were worried. She didn't want her sanctuary disturbed by the likes of Reg Rawlins, medium.

Erin gave a wide yawn, motioning Vic toward the door and herding Reg into the guest room. "You found everything you needed? I'll see you in the morning… you can call or come by the bakery once you're up and around, I assume you won't be when we get up. And don't worry if you think you hear a baby crying or someone being murdered. Erin looked down at Orange Blossom. "I'll try to keep Blossom quiet, but he can be very loud and bothersome. We haven't had a guest before, so I'm not sure how he's going to react. Hopefully, he'll just come and sleep with me like usual and won't bother you."

"He won't bother me," Reg said, though her nostrils flared a little and Erin suspected Reg didn't want anything to do with a cat. "I like cats. He could come and keep me company."

"I'll try to keep him quiet," Erin repeated. She called Orange Blossom to follow her to the bedroom and shut the door most of the way behind him. He could still get out if he wanted to, but she hoped he would just settle in and sleep when she did.

Wednesday, morning Erin was surprised by the delivery of her new freezer. She had the deliveryman put it into position and plugged it in to start it cooling. It was a beautiful, modern-looking steel and glass affair, and Erin could just imagine what it was going to look like filled with frozen treats. While finding gluten-free ice cream and popsicles was not difficult, she would be able to offer the vegans and dairy-allergic and intolerant some lovely dairy-free options.

"That's going to be popular when the heat hits," Vic commented.

Erin, quite warm enough with the late spring weather and the bakery ovens, wiped her forehead with the back of her arm.

"We'll start stocking it tomorrow," she promised.

Vic grinned. Taller than Erin, she didn't have to watch what she ate quite as carefully, and she had a sweet tooth. She would enjoy sampling Erin's new creations.

Terry stopped by in the afternoon for a cookie and a water bottle refill. He leaned on the counter and watched K9 lap water from his bowl.

"So, you got yourself a cold case," he commented.

COUP DE GLACE

Erin breathed in sharply. She had told Terry she wasn't going to look into Grandma Prost's disappearance. How had he found out so quickly that she had agreed to look a little further? Erin hadn't exactly said she would take the case, but she was curious to see what she could find out, just asking around a little and studying Clementine's journal.

"Uh... how did you hear that?"

"Word gets around town pretty quickly," Terry pointed out. Gossip did spread through Bald Eagle Falls like wildfire. All Erin had to do was sneeze, and everyone would be asking her how her cold was for the next three days. "Especially where it involves desserts," Terry added.

Erin stared at him, bewildered.

"Your cold case," he repeated, nodding to the freezer and raising an eyebrow.

"Oh, that!" Erin said with sudden understanding. "Yes, of course. We're going to fill it up with all kinds of tasty desserts."

Terry studied her. "What did you think I was talking about?"

"Nothing. I just didn't connect that you were talking about the freezer."

"What else would I be talking about?" His eyes narrowed as he thought about it. "Don't tell me you've gotten yourself mixed up in another investigation!"

"Well... no... not really. I mean, I don't know that it was a murder. No one is sure what happened. It's probably nothing at all. It's not like I can go back and interview people from twenty years ago."

"Bella's grandmother? I thought you told her no."

"I did, at first, but then... I came across it in Clementine's journal. I was curious when Bella had just been talking about her..."

"Your Aunt Clementine must have been just as big a busybody as you are! What did she write in her journal?"

"I haven't read all of it yet. I might have to pull out the next volume or two, depending on how long things went on before everyone forgot about it."

"You really should just mind your own business."

"I wasn't reading the journal because of Bella's grandma, I was reading it to see what Clementine had to say about my parents and about me. Family history."

"You should just leave it alone."

"Bella wants me to look into it. It isn't like I'm digging around in something that's going to upset people." Erin remembered Bella's concern about her mother not knowing anything about Reg going to the barn to talk to Grandma's ghost and felt a twinge of guilt. Bella wanted Erin to investigate, but Erin had a feeling Bella's mom wouldn't want her to have anything to do with it.

"Erin, no good can come of poking around in old murders. I thought you would have figured that out by now."

"We don't even know it's murder; she just disappeared. She might have left town. Maybe she had a fight with her husband. Maybe she's living the good life in California. It could give the family closure."

His brows drew down. "You know she's not living in California. She would have had some kind of communication with her family by now."

Erin hesitated. "Clementine's journal did kind of assume that she was dead. Either she had passed naturally, or her husband had had something to do with it. But there wasn't enough evidence for the sheriff to get in and have a look around."

"And you think there will be now, twenty years later?"

"No. We're not looking for the police to go in there and tear everything apart. I don't know. I'll talk to Bella. Maybe talk to some people who were around at the time and might know something about what was going on between Grandma and Grandpa. Talk to Bella's mom, if she'll see me. And probably... I won't find anything. Maybe there's nothing to find. But Bella did ask me for help. She's old enough to make her own decision."

"Is she paying you?"

"No, this is just a favor. Doing something for a friend. I don't want anything for it. I'm not a private investigator. I'm just going to have a look. That's all."

K9 had finished his water and his biscuit and sat on his haunches, watching them. Terry signaled K9 to go with him. "I really wish you wouldn't, Erin. I don't think you should be poking your nose into this."

"Don't look now," Vic said, watching a couple of figures approaching the door. "This looks like trouble."

Erin looked to see who it was. Melissa stepped in the door, her dark curls bouncing around her face, smile bright and cheerful. She was followed close behind by Charley.

Charley had the same petite build and pleasant, small facial features as Erin. She had the same dark brown hair and her eyes were the same shape and slant. Beyond that, they could have been strangers. Charley didn't carry herself the same way as Erin, she didn't talk the same way or have the same mannerisms. They weren't cookie cutter copies of each other. Just enough features to be familiar to each other.

Erin had longed for a blood sister when she was a little girl. Maybe she had known that her mother was expecting when she'd had her accident, or maybe it was just a natural fantasy for a lonely child shuttled from one family to another. It was normal for her to want someone like her, someone she had a bond with. Something to anchor her.

But Charley was trouble. She walked in with Melissa, looking like normal and natural friends, maybe a mother-daughter pair, considering the difference in their ages. There was nothing to suggest that Charley had been in an organized crime syndicate. Where Erin had stayed soft, raw from her experiences, Charley had been hardened. She had, as far as Erin could tell, been raised by loving, doting, law-abiding parents, but had rebelled and gone badly off the rails.

Having been kicked out by the Dyson clan after the murder of their heir apparent and their discovery that Charley was blood related to the Jackson clan, Charley had lost her place and position in the Tennessee underworld and was suddenly on her own with no real prospects, except for her half share in The Bake Shoppe, inherited from Trenton Plaint, her brother. She was determined to turn that into a successful venture. Preferably by taking over Davis Plaint's half share as well.

The friendship with Melissa was something new, but it was obvious that they were together and hadn't just shown up at Auntie Clem's at the same time. Erin agreed with Vic that it likely meant trouble.

Pushing all negative thoughts aside, Erin gave the two of them a welcoming smile. "Melissa, Charley! Good to see you again. What can we help you with today?"

"Melissa has been telling me all about her job with the police department," Charley commented. "She's been telling me all about the interesting cases that they've been handling over the last year or so. So many interesting twists and turns!"

Melissa liked to make it sound like she was a police officer herself. In fact, she just helped part time with some of the administrative tasks Clara Jones couldn't keep up with or didn't want to do. Filing, transcription, photocopying. A police department ran on paper. Unfortunately, Erin had been involved in several of those interesting cases over the past year. She didn't exactly want Charley to know all of the details or to think that Erin was some kind of criminal herself.

"Yes, it's been an interesting time in Bald Eagle Falls," Erin agreed, keeping the smile pasted to her face. "I already told you about most of that…"

COUP DE GLACE

"I think you might have left a few things out," Charley returned. She had the look of a mean cheerleader saying something nasty while pretending to be the all-American girl.

Erin looked at the display case. "We've got fresh brownies," she told Melissa. "I know you're always partial to the ones with white chocolate chips."

"Oh, the dominos," Melissa said, zooming in to look at them. "Have you seen these, Charley? They're so good, and they look so classy! Like brownies, that got all dressed up."

Erin nodded, smiling.

Charley looked at Erin for a moment longer, and then joined Melissa in looking over the day's baking and deciding what they wanted. They didn't seem to be there for any take-home baking, just a treat to eat while they visited. Erin rang up their purchases, exchanging a dubious look with Vic. *Just what was Charley up to now?* She wasn't the type to hang out with a more mature woman just for kicks. She might go out for margaritas with her pals back in Moose River, but hanging out with Melissa was something different.

After making their purchases, Melissa and Charley sat down at one of the little tables at the front of the shop to eat and gossip. They weren't loud enough for Erin to make out much of the conversation, but they seemed very chummy and comfortable with each other.

Chapter Nine

WHEN BELLA WAS NEXT covering an afternoon shift, Erin made use of the quieter time between customers to get Bella talking about her family.

"I don't know your mom at all, just to wave and say 'hi' to. What's she like?"

"I don't know. She's pretty strict, I guess. But we get along okay. I know teenage girls and their moms usually have a lot of tensions and arguments, but that's never been us."

"I don't get the feeling that you're particularly rebellious."

Bella grinned. "No. I'm home with her most nights, not out with friends drinking or tipping cows. I have to push sometimes to get her to trust me to handle myself, but I can usually get through to her."

"And no dad in the picture?"

"No. She's never said much about my biological father. She said it was a mistake, that they were never really together. I don't know if that means he was a one night stand, but I kind of get that feeling."

"There are so many kids being raised by single parents, it's not really such a big deal anymore, is it?"

"No. I think if you've got one good parent, you're in pretty good shape. It's the people who don't have anyone they can rely on that I feel sorry for."

COUP DE GLACE

"Yeah." Erin nodded, thinking back to the long list of foster parents she had lived with. Some better, some worse, but no one permanent. No one who would be there for her once she turned eighteen.

"Sorry," Bella said. "I didn't mean you. I just meant... people."

Erin gave her a reassuring smile. "It's okay. Things could have been worse."

"So... yeah. Mom's okay. She can be hard-nosed about things, but she's just trying to protect me."

Erin nodded. "And you don't remember your grandparents at all?"

"No. Grandma was gone before I was born. I guess Grandpa died when I was still a baby. Maybe a year old? I have a picture of him holding me, but I don't actually remember him."

"What did he die of?"

"Just old age, I guess." Bella gave a shrug.

Erin frowned, thinking about it. "Old age? How old is your mom?"

"Uh... not quite fifty."

"Then your grandparents, if they were thirty-something when your mom was born, would be eighty now. But they died when you were a baby; they would have been in their sixties. People don't die of old age in their sixties. Not in this century."

"Oh." Bella thought about that while she moved baked goods around in the display case to fill the empty spaces. "Well, I always thought of them as old. The picture of my grandpa holding me, he looks ancient."

"Your mom never said what he died from?"

"I don't think so. It's not exactly something that comes up in conversation."

"Maybe you could ask her about it. Say your doctor wants to know your family history."

"Yeah, maybe. But Doc has been around here longer than I have. He's probably the one who declared Grandpa dead, if they actually do that in real life."

"Maybe develop an interest in family history? I could show you some of the books my Aunt Clementine pulled together. Naomi at The Book Nook has some genealogy starter sets. You start putting in the names, dates of birth and death, start prompting your mom to tell you what she remembers about them, so you can record it for posterity..."

"I could do that," Bella agreed, brightening. "That would actually be pretty cool. I'd like to have some kind of record. With it just being me and Mom at the farm, I feel sometimes like I don't have any other family. But I know our family has been in Bald Eagle Falls for a long time. I think the farm has been in the family since before the Civil War."

"That's quite a history. Looking through all of the records that Clementine kept has made me view myself and my family differently. I never had any family before I came here, and now... I can look through those books and see generations and generations."

"Maybe you even have some Prosts in your line!"

Erin grinned. "I wouldn't doubt it. You and I could be fifth cousins."

"That would be so cool. I'd love to be related to you."

The bells over the door jangled, and Erin looked over to see Mary Lou coming in.

Mary Lou had always been prim and pressed and presentable. Everything she wore looked like it had been tailored just for her. When Roger's behavior had grown more erratic, Erin had seen Mary Lou looking tired and worn for the first time. Her clothes had not been as neat and carefully presented and Mary Lou had been flustered and irritable.

COUP DE GLACE

Now that Roger was under state care so she could get a good night's sleep again and didn't have to be worrying about what he was doing all the time, Mary Lou once more looked calm and collected; but Erin felt that something about her had changed. It wasn't obvious. Maybe a little more gray in her roots or deeper wrinkles around her mouth. Or maybe it was just the way she held herself, a little more tentative, eyes a little lost or sad.

"Hi, Mary Lou," Erin greeted, putting as much genuine warmth into her voice as she could. She wanted Mary Lou to know that she harbored no bad feelings toward her or Roger. What had happened hadn't been Mary Lou's fault; it hadn't really even been Roger's. It was Joelle's meddling and threats that had triggered Roger's reaction. He would have done just fine living a peaceful life and making the Jam Lady jams and would not have been a threat to any of them if she hadn't gone messing around and making threats. "How are you today? How are your boys?"

"We're all doing better than could be expected," Mary Lou assured her. Her return smile wavered only slightly. "Everything is just fine."

"I'm glad. What can I help you with today? Something for supper, or a treat for your menfolk?"

Mary Lou gazed at the display case. "I should do both. Some of that harvest loaf for lunchboxes. A couple of pizza shells. Maybe some dinner buns? Just plain white?"

Bella went to work packaging it all for Mary Lou.

"And something sweet?" Erin suggested.

Mary Lou let out a breath, her eyes glistening. She stared into the display as if she were facing the most important decision of her life and wasn't quite ready for it. "Erin…"

Erin hurried around the end of the counter to join Mary Lou on the other side. She grasped Mary Lou's arm and gave it a squeeze. "There… it's okay. Everything is going to be fine." She hugged Mary Lou around the shoulders, pulling her close.

"Oh, this is silly." A couple of tears raced down Mary Lou's cheeks, and she rummaged in her handbag for a tissue. "Why can't I make a simple decision?" She found a tissue and dabbed delicately at her eyes, trying not to smear her makeup. "I just feel like… I can't possibly be expected to make one more decision."

"No. No, you shouldn't have to. It can't be easy for you, having to take responsibility for everybody else. How can I help you? Do you want me to just put together a variety box? You know those boys will eat anything, they're not picky about it."

Mary Lou sniffled. She nodded and wiped her nose. "Yes, of course. That would be just fine. Only make sure you put two of each thing—" Mary Lou cut herself off. She frowned and shook her head. "No, don't. The boys are old enough that they can work it out between them who gets what. I don't have to make sure they both have exactly the same thing, do I? That's just silly. What a mother hen I am."

"You're just trying to take care of them and raise them right. You want to be fair to them. They know that."

"Life isn't fair. Maybe that's why I felt like it was so important. Maybe I was trying to make up for life not being fair, us losing everything like we did. But you know what? They're stronger than that. They can certainly navigate through the treacherous waters of choosing their own desserts."

Erin nodded and gave Mary Lou's shoulders another squeeze. She wasn't sure how long she should stay there and comfort Mary Lou, or if she should go back around the counter and package up the treats for the boys. Mary Lou patted Erin's hand.

"You're so sweet, Erin. It must be all the sugar you use. I'm okay now. I don't want to hold you up."

Erin nodded and let go of Mary Lou. She went back around the counter to put together a box of cookies and desserts for Mary Lou's teenagers. "They sure are getting big," she told Mary Lou. "Every time I see them, I marvel at how grown up they look."

Mary Lou nodded. "Oh, yes. They're a big help to me. A comfort to have them around. There are some days when I just can't do anything. I get home from work, and I just want to crawl into bed and pull the blanket up over my head. I freeze up and I just can't function. But they're always there, to help take over and look after their poor mother."

Erin counted out the items in the box.

"Go ahead and make it a baker's dozen," Mary Lou said. "Let them figure out what to do with the last one." Then she hesitated, reconsidering. "Oh, maybe not, maybe just twelve." Then her resolution hardened. "Thirteen. They can figure out whether to share the last one, or negotiate, or just toss it in the garbage. They're almost grown men."

Erin smiled and put the last cookie into the box. "Thirteen, there you go," she announced, before Mary Lou could change her mind again.

Bella looked shyly at Mary Lou. "I've always liked Josh and Campbell," she offered. "They're nice boys, always smiling and friendly. Lots of boys..." Bella looked down at her generous figure, "lots of them can be real jerks. But Campbell and Josh have never been that way. You'd be proud of them."

Mary Lou gave Bella a grateful smile. "Thank you! It's always good to know that they're behaving properly when they're not under mother's watchful eye. You never know what kids are going to behave like when they're not being supervised. You hope they'll do you proud, but you can never be sure!"

Bella blushed slightly. "My mom probably thinks the same thing. But I try to behave like she would want me to." She looked over at Erin, maybe thinking about trying to find out what had happened to her grandmother when her mother so clearly did not want her to. "Mostly, anyway. I try. I wouldn't want her to be ashamed of me."

"I've never seen you do anything that should embarrass your mother," Mary Lou assured her. "I've always thought you were a responsible, mature girl."

Erin went to the register to ring everything up and handed Mary Lou her bags. "There you go. Take care, okay?"

Mary Lou nodded, her eyes glistening again. "I will, Erin. Thank you so much for your help."

The bells jingled as Mary Lou left.

Bella sighed. "That just makes me want to go hug my mom. I've never felt like I am less fortunate because I don't have a dad, but I never thought much about how hard it must have been for my mom to take all that responsibility herself. It couldn't have been easy. Now, I'm all grown up, and she really doesn't have to do anything for me, even if she insists she wants to. But when I was little… for her to work and take care of the farm and raise me all on her own… I never thought about how hard that must have been."

"Well, like you said, she did a good job. And I don't think it's bad that you want to find out more about your grandma and your ancestors. Wanting to know the details about where you came from and what those people were like, that's natural. That's showing that they're important to you. It's not like you're disrespecting your mother." Erin tidied up, even though everything was already neat and laid out properly. "I can tell you… when I was a teenager, I told more than one foster mom 'you're not my real mother.' Like they could help it. Like they weren't just trying to raise someone else's thankless child."

"You couldn't have been that bad," Bella said. "You're so sweet, I can't imagine you ever saying a mean word to anyone."

"Not true, I'm afraid. I've said lots of mean and nasty things in my life. And foster moms definitely took the brunt of it. Foster moms, social workers, teachers, foster sisters…" Erin thought about Reg. How many times had Erin told Reg that she hated her in a fit of teenage pique? How many times had she tried to push Reg away? And why? Because she was annoying? Because she had yet another idea for the two of them to make boatloads of cash? Or was it just teen hormones? Any two hormonal girls living in close quarters with each other would have behaved the same way, blood related or not. "Growing up is hard. I felt so lost and alone and I took it out on whoever was closest."

Bella nodded sagely.

"See what you can find out from your mom," Erin said. "Maybe this whole thing is a way for the two of you to get closer."

Chapter Ten

ERIN TRACED THE LINES in the diary. Clementine's long, looping hand was a little difficult to make out at times, written so closely together that the ascenders and descenders got tangled up with each other.

> Cindy Prost is in town to see what she can do with Ezekiel. I think it was probably Lottie Sturm who got in touch with her, the two of them were always pretty close. Cindy came into the tea room the other day, but seems to be at a complete loss as to what to do with her father. He won't tell her what happened to Martha, insisting that she is still alive and just out of town. Cindy knows very well it isn't true. Martha never left the farm without Ezekiel in her whole life, why would she start now? But she's just at sixes and sevens as to what to do. Ezekiel won't leave the farm and she has no proof that he's done anything wrong or that he's become unbalanced.
>
> Lottie figures Martha is probably buried in the barn or the garden, but there is no way to know for sure. Cindy hasn't come across anything suspicious at the farm other than her mother's absence. Ezekiel seems happy to have Cindy in town and is putting back on some of the weight he has lost since Martha's disappearance. He obviously wasn't eating very much without someone to prepare meals for him. How a grown man can be so helpless, I have no idea. At least my mother always

COUP DE GLACE

taught her boys how to take care of themselves. Even if you get married, there's no guarantee you'll be with that person for the rest of your life or that they'll be able to take care of you.

I suggested to Cindy that if she needed any physical labor done at the farm that her father wasn't doing or wasn't up to, that she give Davis Plaint a call. I think he could use the attention and a little bit of cash to help him out. Trenton always seems to have new clothes, but Davis looks grubby and worn, like he's been sleeping in the rough rather than living at home with his mother and siblings. I've asked the sheriff to check in on the summer house at regular intervals to make sure no one is using it illicitly.

Erin read over the spare account of Bella's mother, Cindy, returning home to take care of Ezekiel.

What was it that made Clementine and apparently Lottie Sturm and Cindy Prost so sure that Martha Prost was dead? If she had died, wouldn't Ezekiel have told someone? Even if he had done something to hurt her, would he really keep insisting that she was alive and well and would be home soon? Was he in denial? Was it the beginning of dementia? Perhaps, like Roger, his behavior had been erratic for some time, and Martha Prost had been doing the best she could to take care of him and to hide his condition from everyone else. Maybe in a moment of anger or confusion he had turned on her but, having hurt her, he couldn't admit to himself what had happened and made up a story to go with it.

Erin wrote down a few notes in her own notebook. Even with Vic's teasing, she couldn't bring herself to keep her notes and lists on her phone rather than hard copy. She was sure that if she put them on her phone, they would end up being erased. Having her thoughts on paper, all neatly marshaled before her, gave Erin a kind of comfort and reassurance. If it was all down in black and white, she wouldn't lose or forget it. She could rest her anxious brain, taking peace in the fact that everything was in proper order.

Lottie Sturm was Cindy's generation, older than Erin. Erin was not close to Lottie, but Lottie did come into the bakery every now and then to pick something up, when she wanted fresh baking and didn't feel like making the trip into the city. Erin had never been favorably impressed with Lottie. She was a mean woman, always out to humiliate Vic or call her down to repentance, to spread some gossip, or otherwise disturb the peace in Bald Eagle Falls. If she had some recollection of what had happened on the Prost farm, some tidbit that Cindy had shared with her or something she had observed herself at the farm, Erin might have to find a way to connect with her.

She wasn't sure she could do that, given the way that Lottie had treated Vic in the past. It felt like a betrayal. Even if she told Vic and Vic understood why she was doing it, Erin wasn't sure she could forgive Lottie's past behavior.

She'd do well to learn a lesson from Melissa and Charley, putting any past differences behind them and apparently enjoying some time together.

There were footsteps behind her, and Erin turned to see Reg coming up the stairs into the attic. For a few minutes, she had actually forgotten that Reg was there.

"Oh, hi Reg."

"Hi yourself. There's a woman here to see you."

Erin looked at the time on her phone. It obviously wasn't Vic, who would have just let herself in and whom Reg had met before. There weren't a lot of other people who would call on Erin in the evening when it was getting so close to her bedtime.

"It must be Adele."

COUP DE GLACE

Erin shut the journal and put it neatly away. She followed Reg back down the stairs. After pushing the stairs back up into the ceiling, she went out to the living room. It was indeed Adele. She looked uncomfortable to be waiting for Erin in the living room. She often made a cup of tea for Erin before bed, and the formality of waiting like a guest didn't suit her.

"Erin, I didn't know you had company. I'm sorry to interrupt you."

"No, not at all. Adele, this is Reg. She's just staying here for a few days while she looks for a place of her own. She's... thinking of moving to Bald Eagle Falls. Reg, this is Adele." Erin wasn't sure how to introduce Adele. As her groundskeeper? Her tenant? "A friend of mine."

"I think I've heard your name in town," Reg said slowly, looking Adele up and down with a suspicious, cat-like gaze.

Adele was obviously also taking Reg's measure. Reg didn't like to go to bed as early as Erin and hadn't yet changed for bed, which meant she was still in her fortune-teller costume, looking ready to run a carnival booth at a moment's notice.

"What is it you do?" Adele asked baldly. "Are you... a practicer of the arts?"

Erin looked from one friend to the other, the tension drawing out between them.

Reg gave a dramatic, mysterious smile. "Are you a kindred spirit, maybe?"

Adele wasn't in costume. She didn't wear costumes. But she did tend to wear long, flowing dresses and a hooded cloak. Her skin had a pale, ageless cast to it. To Erin, Adele looked just like she would have expected a modern witch to look. But as most of Bald Eagle Falls hadn't immediately identified her as one, Erin figured she was biased by her prior knowledge.

Adele raised her eyebrows at Reg's flamboyant outfit. "Perhaps *not*."

"I'm a medium. I foretell the future, read palms, communicate with the dead, whatever my clients need."

"Your clients? So you do this for recompense?"

"If you've got it, you might as well use it. You don't use your... talents to support yourself?"

"I sell some crafts and herbs," Adele said slowly. "My... faith... is not for sale."

Reg snorted. "Oh, you're very good," she said admiringly. "I'd almost believe it. A girl can't expect things to just fall into her lap these days. We have to take care of ourselves, don't we? You sound like a real soul sister." Reg looked over at Erin. "I might have known you wouldn't drift that far from your roots. You give me a big lecture about how you don't scam people, but your close friend is doing just the same thing we always did. Not quite as high and mighty as you were pretending, are you?"

Erin looked over at Adele, worried she was going to be offended. An attack by Erin's guest might as well be an attack by Erin herself. She was worried Adele would think that Erin had been talking about her, but Erin always avoided any mention of Adele and what she was or wasn't.

"Are you aware of the power you are playing with?" Adele asked Reg. "Do you really know what forces a medium employs?"

Erin didn't believe in magic or sorcery or any other unseen powers, whether they were those discussed by Adele or by one of Erin's Christian friends. She believed what she could see and hear and touch. And Reg didn't believe it either. She might pretend to for her scam, but she knew there wasn't actually anything to it.

Reg laughed. "You're even better than I thought. I know my 'powers,' don't you worry about that. I know exactly what I'm doing. People will see and believe what they want to."

COUP DE GLACE

Adele shook her head. She made a slight movement toward the door. "If you play with fire, you are going to get burned. Don't say I didn't warn you."

Adele gave Erin a nod and left the house. Erin wanted to hurry after Adele and reassure her that she was not mixed up in Reg's hocus-pocus. Just because Reg was staying in Erin's house, that didn't mean Erin agreed with her about anything. They were just sisters, and Reg had called in a sister's privilege. Erin shook her head at Reg.

"You were not very nice to my friend," she snapped. All at once, she was fifteen and furious over Reg getting her in trouble yet again. "I would expect better from a house guest. But I guess you don't understand southern hospitality. You don't know how to treat a sister; how would you know how to treat my friend?" Erin's eyes burned with angry tears and her throat constricted. "I expected better from you, Regina Rawlins!"

Reg withdrew into herself, shrinking before Erin's eyes. She ducked her head and looked ashamed. "I wasn't trying to insult your friend." Under Erin's stern gaze, she turned pink. "Okay, maybe I was. I just thought… she shouldn't have… okay, I shouldn't have behaved that way. I was rude to your friend. I'll apologize the next time I see her, okay? I'm sorry."

"You're the guest here. You should know how to behave. I did you a favor putting you up. I didn't have to do that. I could have sent you back to the city to find a motel."

"But you wouldn't—Yes, okay, you could have. I didn't think you would be able to turn out your own sister, but you could have just said no, and you probably wanted to. I'll try to be a more gracious guest."

"You'd better," Erin agreed. "Or you'll find yourself out in the street, middle of the night or not."

"Well…" Reg looked at the wall clock ticking away. "It's actually not exactly the middle of the night."

Erin froze her with another stare.

"Okay. It's the middle of the night for you. So I'd better let you get to bed."

Erin glanced to the back of the house. She hadn't had tea with Adele. What about bread and jam with Vic? It was getting late, and Erin should be getting to sleep instead of looking for other things to do. "Yes, I'd better do that. You're in for the night, right?"

Reg shrugged. "There isn't exactly a night life in Bald Eagle Falls, is there? You chose a pretty sleepy town to live in. I wouldn't have pegged you for the quiet life."

If only it were. In the past year, Erin had learned not to take the quiet persona of Bald Eagle Falls at face value. There was always something more sinister bubbling beneath the surface.

"Goodnight," she told Reg. "Keep out of trouble."

"Who, me?" A smile of mischief spread over Reg's face. "What kind of trouble would I get into?"

Chapter Eleven

BELLA'S TENTATIVE INVITATION TO go out to the Prost farm came that Friday, much sooner than Erin had expected. She had figured it would take at least a week or two for Bella to dither around and find a time Reg could put on a show of visiting with Grandma.

Covering up the phone mic, Reg explained to Erin that Bella wanted both of them to go to the farm together. She knew Erin and trusted her judgment and her ability to figure out what had happened twenty years earlier. Erin hesitated, then agreed. While she didn't want to go out at the same time as Reg and appear to be sanctioning her talking to spirits, she didn't know when Bella would be able to arrange for her to go out again. And if she went along with Reg, she could keep an eye on her sister and make sure she didn't go overboard.

"Do you need directions?" Reg asked and, when Erin nodded, Reg got driving instructions for the Prost farm. They would head over in the early evening, when Cindy was going into the city for a doctor's appointment and to run some errands.

"Now you remember she's already scared of ghosts," Erin told Reg sternly once she was off the phone. "I don't want you making her worse. You want to convince her that Grandma's spirit is at peace and no longer haunting the barn, got it?"

Reg sighed. "Fine. You know there'd be more repeat business if we drew it out, though."

"We don't want repeat business. We want to help a friend. And you are not going to charge her."

"What? How am I supposed to make the money to get out on my own if you won't let me charge her?"

"This is a favor," Erin repeated.

"Fine. Hopefully, she'll spread the word to all of her friends, and we'll get business out of her that way." Reg scowled. "It's not very hospitable of you to say I can't even earn a living."

"Nice try," Erin told her, unconcerned. Hospitality only stretched so far.

The Prost farm was farther out of town than Erin had expected. She had thought that it would be one of the houses clinging to the outskirts of Bald Eagle Falls, but it was another half hour of driving before they got to the access road. There were three mailboxes at the turnoff from the highway, suggesting to Erin that there were several farms down the road. The Prost farm was, luckily, the first, so they didn't have to rattle their teeth going over the washboard road any farther.

Erin pulled into the graveled clearing in front of the house, where there were vehicles of varying vintages parked or abandoned. Several of them looked like they had been there for decades.

Bella came out of the yellow and white farmhouse that had to be at least a hundred years old. If the Prost family had been on the mountain since before the Civil War, who knew how old it was or how many different farmhouses had stood on the same patch of ground over the past two hundred years.

Bella gave a jerky wave. Erin parked the Challenger and got out. It was obvious on approaching Bella that she was nervous. Maybe she was having second thoughts about having them over. Most likely, about having Reg over.

COUP DE GLACE

"Uh, hi Erin. Reg. This is… so weird. I can't believe I'm doing this. Do you really think I should? Maybe I should just leave it alone. Wait until Mom is ready to tell me about her parents. Maybe what happened to Grandma isn't really the point. Maybe it's just learning about them and the rest of my ancestors."

"If that's what you want," Erin agreed.

Reg gave Erin an irritated look. "I thought you wanted some peace," she told Bella. "Are you going to get peace from a restless ghost just talking about what she used to be like? You could just wait to see if it goes away, but usually restless spirits don't get quieter over time. They just get more insistent. They want the living to pay attention to them when they have something to say."

"Yeah." Bella nodded. Erin could tell she was clenching her jaw, steeling herself for what was to come.

"Maybe we can just visit in the parlor for a few minutes first. Did you find any books or old albums with family pictures?"

"Actually, yes." Bella motioned for Erin and Reg to enter the house with her. Reg glared at Erin.

"Quit trying to sabotage me," she hissed.

"I'm not! I'm just trying to help Bella. I'm not here to put on a show. I'm here to help a friend work through a loss."

"A loss? Her grandma died before she was born. She's not suffering from a loss, believe me."

"It's still a loss. Whether you remember or not, it hurts to lose a loved one."

Reg shook her head stubbornly. They followed Bella into the house.

The interior had been updated, but it was obvious that it was an old building that had been through several renovations and refittings. The big panel TV on the wall was at odds with the rustic interior. There was modern furniture mixed with old hand-turned wooden pieces. There was a startling contrast between the scarred coffee table that had been worn down with hundreds of hands and boots over the years, and the tablet computer laying on top of it.

"Home, sweet home," Bella said, making a wide motion to indicate the house.

"It's very homey," Erin said.

"Have a seat. I'll show you the albums."

Erin and Reg made themselves comfortable at opposite ends of the couch, and Bella sat between them. She flipped through the thick pages of the book, browsing through the faded pictures showing her grandparents, her mother as a little girl, and then eventually a picture of Grandpa holding baby Bella in his lap. He looked much older than he had in the other pictures, thin, his hair sparse, eyes distant behind his glasses. He had just a hint of a smile on his face, looking down at his granddaughter.

"Weren't you just the cutest baby," Erin said. "That's a sweet picture."

Bella ducked her head. "Thank you."

"Did you ask your mom anything about your grandparents since we talked?"

"No, not really. She saw me looking through the albums, and I asked her if she missed them, but…"

"I'm sure she misses them, even after so many years."

Bella nodded. "She said she did. She said she wasn't that much older than me when she lost them," Bella's brows drew down. "But she must have been… in her thirties. Almost twice my age."

Reg laughed. "It's all relative. She means she was too young to lose them, that she wasn't ready to be independent and all on her own so soon."

Bella looked impressed. "Yeah, I guess. I wouldn't want to be all on my own now, either. I've still got so much to learn… and I want to go to college…"

"What do you want to study?" Erin asked.

COUP DE GLACE

"Business management. I'd like to get an MBA, but I probably won't be able to do that right away. Need to make some money before I can afford to get a masters."

"Wow. That's quite an undertaking. Not a lot of women go into business administration."

"I think it would be really cool," Bella enthused. "I've always been interested in how businesses work and all of the financial formulas and benchmarks." She shrugged awkwardly. "And baking. I like that too."

"Sounds like you're set to cook the books," Reg offered.

Bella giggled. "No way, I'm not getting involved in anything shady. I'll only use my powers for good."

The conversation gradually petered out, and Erin was trying to figure out how to tactfully ask Bella for more information about her grandmother, and maybe a tour around the property and the barn. There wasn't much she could get from sitting on the couch looking at old photos.

"Do you have anything that belonged to your grandma?" Reg asked. "I think it's time..."

Bella turned a shade paler. She'd been relaxing and having a good time and was maybe trying to convince herself that she wasn't actually going to have to deal with her grandmother's ghost.

"Something that belonged to her? I don't know..."

"Maybe an article of clothing? Jewelry? Hairbrush? Your mom must have kept some of her things."

Bella thought about it for a minute, then nodded. "Uh... yeah. My mom has this locket that used to be Grandma's. It even has a lock of her hair in it, from when she was a baby."

"Perfect. That makes it even better."

Bella didn't move.

"Go get it," Reg encouraged.

"It's in my mom's room."

"Okay."

"I'm... not supposed to get into her stuff."

Reg scowled. "What are you, two? You're not messing anything up. You're just borrowing it for a few minutes to enhance our chances of speaking to your Grandma. Your mom would want that for you. You're not keeping it, and neither am I. It's going to go right back into the jewelry box when we're done, and she'll never know the difference."

"I don't think she would want me to."

"Of course she would. She wouldn't want to take away an opportunity for you to know your grandma. Never."

"Well..."

"Come on. Tell her, Erin. It's not going to hurt anything for her to borrow her grandma's necklace for a few minutes."

Before Erin could open her mouth to answer, Reg was already talking over her. Maybe she had anticipated that Erin wouldn't be quite so quick to tell Bella to disobey what she knew her mother would want her to do.

"Why don't I go up with you? You can show me where it is, and you won't even have to touch it. Maybe I'll be able to feel something more when I go into her bedroom. Is she in the master bedroom where your grandmother used to sleep?"

Bella was looking a little dazed as Reg got to her feet and encouraged Bella to stand and take Reg to the bedroom.

"Yes, the master bedroom. It's really not any bigger than the other bedrooms, but that's where grandma and grandpa slept, and probably their parents too, for generations."

With more encouragement from Reg, Bella walked with her to the bedroom to get the necklace. Erin stood up as well and walked around the room looking out the windows and studying the various pictures and knickknacks. It was only a couple of minutes before Reg was returning with Bella, waving the old locket at Erin.

"Got it. We're going to head out to the barn."

COUP DE GLACE

Bella caught Reg's arm. "Do we have to go out to the barn? Can't we just do it here? It's more comfortable, and you've got the locket, so you can call her, right?"

"This is a complex process, Bella. You can't oversimplify things. It's not just like dialing someone up on the phone. If the place that your grandma has been haunting is the barn, then that's where we need to go. Where her energy will be the strongest."

"But I don't really even know if she is. I mean… she might be… but maybe it's somebody else, who's been haunting it for years. Maybe there's something else going on. I don't know for sure that Grandma…"

"Quit being such a scaredy cat," Reg snapped. "Just pull yourself together and come. This is what we're here for."

Cowed, Bella followed along behind Reg. Erin caught up to them and put her arm around Bella.

"It's okay. I don't think there's anything to be scared of. And you can always change your mind. If you don't want to do this, then just tell Reg. Stand up to her and don't let her run over you."

"No…" Bella's voice was small. "She's right. I keep trying to find excuses not to do this, when I know it's what I want. What I need. It's just so frustrating… to want something and to be scared of it at the same time."

"I know."

They followed Reg toward the barn in silence. It was a big red affair, just like on TV and all the picture postcards. But as they got closer to it, Erin saw that it had fallen into disrepair. The wood sagged and buckled. It hadn't been painted in a long time. There were no sounds of animals coming from it.

"What do you farm?" she asked.

"Goats," Bella advised, giving Erin a smile. "Milk, meat, hair, hide. Everything but the bleat, my mom says."

"Where are they?"

Bella moved forward to help Reg to open the barn doors.

"Not in here. They're in the pasture right now. When we bring them in, it's to a more modern barn back there. This one—" She grunted as she pulled the doors open, "—isn't being used anymore."

Chapter Twelve

STEPPING INTO THE SHADOW of the old building, Erin felt a chill. Just the results of being out of the blazing sun. Nothing to be scared of. They were all quiet as Reg led the way into the barn. Bella seemed paralyzed at first. Erin could see the panic in her eyes. She wasn't going in there. The whole point of Reg and Erin being there was to rid the barn of the ghost so that Bella could go in there. She had no intention of going in until the ghost was gone.

Reg spun in a slow circle as if trying to pick up the ghost's psychic vibrations. Erin rolled her eyes. She knew it was all for show. She hoped Bella wasn't actually falling for it. She was a smart girl with a good head on her shoulders, if she'd just stop being scared of spooks.

"Grandma…" Reg called in a low, faint voice. "Grandma Prost, are you here…?"

There was a sudden flapping of wings and Erin jumped. She looked up into the barn's rafters, fully expecting to see them lined with bats, but they were not. Instead, there were birds. They were disturbed by the visitors, but they didn't all rush out in a cloud of mad flapping and shrieking. A few flew out. Others fluttered around, alighting here and there, not settling back in. Others simply eyed the visitors with cold, black eyes and then ignored them.

"Creepy," Bella muttered. "It's all too creepy."

"It's nothing," Erin said lightly, though her heart was still thrumming too fast in her chest, "it's just a few birds. Nothing to be scared of."

Reg walked around, eyes closed, the locket clasped between two hands and held over her head. Whether or not her little haint Geiger counter was supposed to be working or not, Erin didn't know. Reg didn't say whether she could feel the ghost there.

"Grandma Prost," Reg intoned again, "Bella is here to talk to you. She wants to commune with you and to know why you haunt this place. Can you give us a sign that you hear us?"

More flapping of wings distracted Erin from other potential signs. She forced herself to ignore the birds and the overwhelming ammonia smell of their guano, and to look around the barn. There were pieces of equipment that she didn't recognize, that had been sitting there rusting for a long time. Other hand and garden tools that she recognized. A thick layer of dust and frosting of bird excrement over everything made it look as if it had been standing empty for generations, not just since Cindy had returned to her childhood home.

"How long since it has been used?" Erin asked Bella.

"What? Oh, the barn? I don't really know. Not since I can remember. I don't think it was ever used for the goats." Bella poked her head in the door and looked around with more interest and a little less fear. "No, this isn't outfitted for goats. Mostly this is equipment for clearing and gardening."

Erin took a couple of steps so that she was inside the barn. She didn't walk in very far, not wanting to risk a bird taking aim at her head. There was an ancient fridge or freezer on one wall. More garden implements. Some dangerous-looking knives that Erin assumed were for clearing brush or hand-cutting crops. They hadn't been used for a long time, but Erin figured they were probably still sharp enough to do damage. She hoped that Grandma hadn't been killed with something like that. It was hard enough to deal with a death in the family, without it being by gory violence.

Reg saw the direction of Erin's eyes and started walking toward the knives, arms outstretched as if groping in the dark.

"I feel something. It's… drawing me this way…"

"No, it's not," Erin snapped. "It's definitely coming from the other way."

Bella's eyes got wider. "Do you feel it too?" she asked eagerly.

Erin shook her head, but her eyes were on Reg. She didn't want Reg putting any thoughts in Bella's brain. Not thoughts of violent or bloody death.

Reg stopped, then backed up a little, acknowledging Erin's dictates on the matter. She could have told a good story with the knives, but she would find something else instead.

"Grandma Prost… come join me, Bella, it will be stronger if we can magnify the pull by both of us being close together."

"No, I'm just going to stay out here."

"Come inside, Bella. You need to be in here. You have Prost blood and I don't. She wants to know that a member of her family is here, and it isn't just someone trying to fool her."

Erin wanted to ask who would be trying to fool a ghost, but bit her lip and kept her comments to herself.

Bella wavered, her toes just over the line formed by the doors. "I'll just look in. I can see from here."

"Come in. Nothing is going to hurt you. Why would your grandmother do anything to hurt you?"

"I've seen *Poltergeist*. Ghosts are fed by feelings. They take all of the negative feelings from the air around them, and they use their power to make things happen. To hurt people."

"What bad feelings, Bella?" Erin asked softly. "Are there a lot of bad feelings around the farm? In the barn?"

Reg's eyes flickered over to Erin. She liked the role Erin was playing, acting as Bella's confidante. Providing balance to Reg's role.

"No," Bella said, forcing a laugh. "What bad feelings would there be in the barn? No one has used it in years. And the farm has been my home, where I've been loved and cherished. It's not a bad place."

"Then you don't think there are any bad feelings for a ghost to feed on?"

Bella frowned. She looked quickly around the barn. "No, nothing bad happened here. It was just shut up after Grandma died."

"Why?"

"Because..." Bella made a helpless gesture. "Because they did, I don't know why."

Erin walked around the edge of the wall, exploring a little further. "Did your grandma garden? Were these things hers?"

"I don't know. Maybe."

On a workbench, Erin could make out a bundle of cloth with a flower print. A gardening smock? An old men's shirt that Grandma could pull on over her dress when she didn't want to chance getting it dirty? Erin didn't touch it. Just made note of it and went on. "There's nothing to be worried about here," she told Bella. "You can come in."

Bella tentatively took one step into the barn. She looked around, eyes wild, expecting something bad to happen the instant she set foot inside.

"See?" Erin prompted. "Nothing to worry about."

Like Erin, Bella didn't seem to want to walk under the rafters full of birds.

"Your grandmother's spirit is strong here," Reg announced. She stood absolutely still, then her eyes rolled back in her head so that only the sightless whites showed.

COUP DE GLACE

Her face was a mask. Bella gave a little shriek and grabbed Erin's arm for stability.

"It's okay." Erin wanted to tell Bella that it was all just an act. She and Reg had spent many hot summer afternoons trying to come up with the worst, scariest faces possible. Inside-out eyelids, cheeks puffed out, tongue dangling lifelessly… they had come up with some pretty gruesome ones. Reg's eyeball rolling was just the beginning.

"What do you want to say to your grandmother?" Reg asked in her spookiest rasp.

"I don't know. Nothing. I don't want anything."

"Why would you disturb my rest without a reason? You must have had a reason!" Reg's voice was not her own. It was a good approximation of a Tennessee accent. The low, gravelly quality covered up any imperfections or slip-ups. It was the shaky voice of an old woman. But one who had just awakened from the grave? For some reason, Erin didn't think so.

Bella was rooted to the spot. "I'm sorry… I just wanted to… I just wanted to make sure you knew that you were loved. That people cared when you disappeared. Grandpa too. Mom said he was really broken up about it. He just went downhill the years after you were gone. He wasn't ever the same. Whatever happened… he mourned you. He did."

"Where is he? Where is Ezekiel?"

"He's… in the cemetery. There's a plot there… for you too. But we never had a body to bury…"

"Why didn't you bury me?"

"We didn't know what happened to you. It was before I was born. I don't know. Nobody wants to tell me about it."

"It's so cold here," Reg drew the words out, "why is it so cold?"

"I don't know. Cold in here? Is that what you mean?"

"It's so cold." Reg wrapped her arms around her body. She swayed back and forth. "It's so cold and cramped in here. Please let me out."

"In here?" Bella spoke urgently. "Where? Where are you? I'll make them take you out and put you in the grave beside Grandpa's, if you'll show me where you are. I'll take care of it. Then you won't need to haunt the barn any more, and we'll all be happy."

"I've been so cold for so long..."

Bella covered her mouth. She stumbled backward, out the barn doors again. She took a deep breath and continued to retreat, until she was in the sun. She lifted her face up toward it, eyes closed, letting it beat down on her face and warm her. Erin followed her out, worried she was going to faint if she tried to go back to the house on her own.

"It's okay, Bella. Bella, it's just Reg. There isn't any—"

"There isn't any reason to be scared," Reg covered easily, reaching them. "She's restless and confused, but she isn't malevolent. You can understand how confused she is, can't you?"

Bella nodded. She lowered her face and opened her eyes to look at Reg. "I'm confused, so I can only imagine how hard it would be for someone who didn't even have a brain to sort it out. Can you imagine being alive one minute, and the next thing you know, you're dead? You can't do any of the normal things anymore. You can't talk to the people you love. You just watch everything going on without you."

Reg looked impressed. This mark had a good imagination, even if she did lean more toward finances than storytelling.

"I think that with another session or two, we'll be able to figure out what's bothering your grandma and to sort it all out—"

"No." Bella's hand closed around the locket that Reg held in her hand, and she took it away. "No more. I didn't know if this was a good idea from the start, and now I know it's not. My mom would be horrified if she saw what you were doing in there. We're good Christian people, we don't go around communing with the dead."

Reg blinked in surprise at this. "Plenty of Christians commune with the dead," she protested. "Seances and Ouija boards and other methods of communication, they're just as big with Christians as with pagans and mystics."

"No," Bella shook her head emphatically. "No more. I don't feel right about this."

There was a loud snap in the trees beside the barn, a brittle branch someone or something had stepped on that sounded like a gunshot in their ears, their nerves stretched taut by Reg's performance.

Bella grabbed Erin's arm. They all looked as one in the direction it had come from.

"Who's there?" Bella demanded. "Who's back there?"

Chapter Thirteen

THEY ALL WAITED, STRAINING for another sound. Erin thought she could hear the soft rustling of footsteps. The wind was rushing through the leaves and there were birds calling back and forth to one another, all of the little wilderness noises competed with each other so she wasn't sure what she could hear.

"Is someone there?" Bella demanded again, her voice loud in the stillness.

Erin and Reg looked at each other. The three of them started moving, slowly and as quietly as possible, into the trees that grew right up to the walls of the barn. Erin scanned back and forth, searching for the shape of a person or maybe a deer in the thick growth. The smell of the grasses and weeds they crushed under their feet as they walked was fresh and pungent. Everything seemed peaceful, but Erin's guts churned, her heart thudded hard and fast, and her muscles were bunched, ready to run.

They didn't see anyone else. The property was isolated, and Erin couldn't imagine that anyone was out walking in the woods. It had to be an animal. A random noise. That was all. They stood there, looking around, for a few minutes. Bella was scanning the ground, but apparently didn't see anything that was worth pointing out to Erin and Reg.

"That was weird," she said breathlessly.

"You haven't had that happen before?" Reg asked.

Bella shifted uneasily. "I try to stay away from the barn," she said. "It always freaks me out. Mom said—" She cut herself off abruptly, frowning.

"Your mom said what?" Erin prompted.

"She's always told me to stay away from the barn," Bella said.

Erin was sure that wasn't what she'd been about to say. "Why?" Had Cindy said that it was dangerous in there with all of the equipment? It wasn't necessarily a great place for a young child to be hanging around. Or was she the one who had planted the seed in Bella's mind that it was haunted?

Bella shook her head. "I don't know," she said abruptly. "She just told me to stay away from here." She looked around once more. "This is creeping me out. Let's go back to the house."

They made their way back the way they had come through the trees. There was a blur of motion from a tree right beside her, and Bella shrieked and threw her hands up in front of her face to protect herself. It was Erin who recovered first.

"It was just a cat," she said, looking at the sleek, silver gray form that had stopped at the edge of the clearing and was looking back at them, clearly as spooked by them as they were by it.

"Oh!" Bella let out a whoosh of breath. "Thank goodness! I though the ghost was going to get me for sure!"

"Here, puss!" Erin called softly. She made kissing noises, trying to call it over like she did with Orange Blossom. "Come here. Come see us."

"We have a lot of feral cats around here. They aren't tame," Bella explained. "There are one or two of the mommas that will come up to you, but not that one. I've seen it around once or twice. It's pretty wild."

Erin made a few more noises. The cat watched her, then eventually slunk away, disappearing into the trees.

> Cindy was expecting Davis to be by today to help with the farm and called me to find out if I had seen or heard from him. If the boy wants to hold down a job, he needs to be more reliable! There are too many days that he sleeps in or "isn't feeling well enough to work." I hate to unjustly accuse him of doing drugs, but I'm afraid that may be the case.
>
> But today it was not his fault. This time it was Trenton. He had a serious allergic reaction and Davis drove him at breakneck speeds—without a license, I might add—to the city hospital to get him emergency treatment. The doctors said that Trenton was lucky to make it in time; he might easily have died on the way. Apparently, he is allergic to soybeans. He's lucky he had his brother to look out for him.

Curled up in the living room with the two animals for company, Erin read and re-read the journal entry. There was the proof in black and white that Davis knew about his brother's allergy to soy. It might not be proof that he and Joelle had conspired to murder Trenton, but it was close. It would shore up the case being developed against Davis. Throughout the journal, there were a number of underlines and annotations that Erin had come to believe Joelle had made while the journal had been in her possession. She had marked little bits of knowledge and gossip that she planned to use in her blackmail campaign. There was a margin bracket marking the passage about Trenton's allergy attack, with a little smiley face beside it. Erin felt a rush of anger at Joelle over her callousness. A smile for the fact that Trenton had had a life-threatening allergy that she had used to kill him? Even if it could be argued that Joelle hadn't intentionally killed Trenton, the smile removed any doubt that she had been happy about the result. The woman really was cold-blooded.

"I have to say I'm not unhappy that you are gone," she told Joelle aloud.

Orange Blossom and Marshmallow both looked up at the sound of her voice.

"Not one bit," Erin reiterated, shaking a scolding finger at the absent party to emphasize her point. The animals looked at her for a moment longer, then went back to napping.

There was the sound of a door slamming behind the house, and Erin looked up, frowning. In a few moments, there was a soft knock at the back door.

"Come on in," Erin called.

She was a little surprised when Willie poked his head in the back door. She'd been expecting Vic, though Vic would not have knocked.

"It's me. Are you decent?"

"As decent as I'm going to get. Come in."

Willie slunk into the kitchen, closing the door behind him. He looked at the burglar alarm panel. "You should have this armed. What's the point of having a burglar alarm if you don't use it?"

"I'll arm it before I go to bed and when I go to the bakery in the morning. Just like always. It didn't exactly stop my last burglar."

"No… I suppose that's true."

Willie stomped into the living room and slumped into one of the easy chairs. Erin didn't say anything about Willie's apparently grimy face and hands and whether he was going to get her furniture dirty. She knew from experience that his skin was stained dark from the mining and refining work that he did. It wasn't going to wash out, it was like a permanent tattoo.

"What is it about women?" Willie demanded.

"I don't know. What happened?"

"Why can't a woman just accept it when her partner tries to do something nice? Why do they have to suspect your motives and argue about it and act like you're just doing something to irritate them? It doesn't make any sense!"

Erin closed the journal and put it to the side. Orange Blossom yawned, stretched, and curled up the opposite direction. "What did Vic say?"

"I'm doing this for her! I want her to have a good, stable life. I want her to be happy. I want her to know she can rely on me. Why can't she just accept that? Why is she fighting me?"

"About what?"

Willie snorted and lapsed into silence, folding his arms across his chest. Erin waited.

"I don't know what you two are actually arguing about, unless you tell me."

"I'm sure she's talked to you about it already."

Erin thought back over what Willie had said and anything Vic might have said that was related the last couple of weeks.

"Oh. About you getting a regular job."

Willie nodded. "It's not like I'm not bringing in good money right now, but it ebbs and flows, and I can never predict how much I'm going to have in any particular month. Women want stability. A predictable flow so that they can save and plan household expenses. No one wants to be left not knowing whether there's going to be five dollars or five thousand dollars coming in during a given month. A salaried job gives you that. A regular, predictable income."

"Until it doesn't," Erin pointed out. "You get downsized or get fired or quit. Or a huge expense comes up that you weren't planning on and you have to figure out how to pay for it."

COUP DE GLACE

"Obviously that stuff can still happen." Willie flapped his hand to wave it all away. "But at least with a regular, salaried position, you have some expectations."

Erin let a few breaths pass in silence. "But that's not what Vic wants."

"It's so maddening!" Willie huffed. "I go to all of this work to try to change my lifestyle to something more suited to a long-term relationship and shared household, and she doesn't appreciate it at all! In fact, you'd think I had offended her by suggesting she deserves a partner who can provide a steady income!"

"Maybe she didn't want anything to change. Maybe she doesn't actually mind the way you work at several different projects at once."

Willie stared at Erin. "I should have known you'd automatically be on her side. Vic deserves to have someone who can take care of her properly."

"Maybe she doesn't want to be taken care of. She does already have her own job and her own place. She's not looking for someone to come rescue her. She's looking for someone to spend time with her and cherish her."

"That's what having a proper job would do. I wouldn't have to go away to deal with out-of-town projects. I wouldn't be off at the mines by myself, with her wondering if I was safe. I'd be there for her."

Erin raised her brows and shifted her position, bothering Orange Blossom. "You wouldn't even continue your mining on the side? You'd close the mines? Sell your claims?"

He spread his hands apart in a dramatic shrug, like that should have been obvious. "She wouldn't have to worry anymore. I'd be working a safe office job, home with her during the evenings and weekends. Isn't that what she wants?"

"I don't know. What did she say to you?"

"She said she liked me just the way I am."

Erin laughed at how exasperated he sounded. "Well, maybe she does!"

"But that's stupid! There are already enough differences between us without her having to worry about where I am, if I'm safe, and how much money I'll bring home. She should be happy that I'm willing to change for her."

"Would you want her to change the kind of person she is? Maybe you'd like her to be the kind of person who shrieks at spiders and needs a big strong man to protect her from all of life's disappointments and inequalities. Maybe you'd like her to be home all day instead of working, just waiting for you to finish your new office job and make her feel fulfilled."

Willie opened his mouth to snap back at her. He closed his mouth and scowled.

"Don't you want her to be a fragile little homemaker?" Erin persisted. "That's what all men want isn't it? Someone to protect?"

"I'd never want Vic to turn into something like that. I'd never want her to think that she has to pretend to be something else just to make me happy."

"Maybe that's not what she wants from you either."

"But I'm not talking about… I mean, she shouldn't have to…" Willie blew out his breath. He sat there for a few moments, stewing and occasionally sputtering out a few words of protest.

"Is that what I'm doing?" he demanded finally.

Erin shrugged. "I don't know. Is it?"

"Well… I didn't *know* I was."

She laughed.

Willie swore and pushed himself up out of his chair. "Don't ask me why I should apologize for trying to be nice and be a good provider," he growled.

He marched back out of the house. Erin saw his silhouette cross the yard to the garage and climb the stairs. She couldn't hear his knock, but saw the sliver of light as the door opened and stayed open just an inch or two while Willie talked to Vic, before she finally opened it the rest of the way and let him in.

Vic was in a better mood the next morning than she had been for several days. Erin eyed her as they mixed and poured batters, getting ready for the day ahead.

"I gather you and Willie came to an understanding?"

Vic laughed. "I thought he was gone for good last night. I mean, not forever, but for the night. I never expected him to come back telling me that he'd been wrong and maybe he should have asked me what I wanted before he decided to go and make a big life change like that." Vic shook her head. "Nothing like an abject apology to improve a relationship!"

"You guys have certainly had your ups and downs. I'm glad Willie decided he could see your point of view. That's the first step!"

"I could see *his* point of view all along. It's just that it was wrong."

Erin laughed and started spooning out dollops of filling into tart shells from the freezer. "In your humble opinion."

"It's my opinion, all right. Humble it is not."

"I gather."

"Thanks for talking to him. It was good for him to have someone else to talk to about it. He doesn't really have a lot of friends around here, and I don't know what any of his guy friends would have told him. He needed to hear a woman's perspective."

"Glad to help. Do you want to return the favor and do something for me?"

"Sure," Vic agreed, without waiting to hear what it was.

"You could really get yourself into trouble, agreeing without knowing what it is first!"

Vic shrugged. She wiped a smear of flour off her chin with the back of her wrist. "It's not like you're going to ask me to murder my grandmother. It's probably not even anything very big. I know you."

"I need someone to go with me when I go out to the Prost farm again to interview Cindy. I don't want to do it alone."

"Why don't you take Terry with you? He wouldn't let anything happen to you."

"Terry and I... don't exactly see eye to eye on this. I haven't told him I'm going out there, and I don't think he'd be too happy if he knew."

Vic *tsked*, shaking her head. "Here you are, fixing my relationship, and running yours into the crapper. I think sooner or later Officer Terry Piper is going to have to realize that you've got a mind of your own and he isn't going to be able to stop you from looking into every crime that happens in your area code."

"It's not that bad. And I'm not going to keep looking into other crimes, this is just... once. For a friend."

"Mm-hmm." Vic did not sound convinced.

"So will you?"

Vic gave her batter a stir. "Come out with you? Sure. I'll tag along."

"Good! I appreciate it. And if Terry knew, he'd be happy you were coming with me too."

"Do I need to bring my gun? Keep an eye out for any dangerous varmints?"

"I don't think so! There were a lot of birds in the barn and a cat scared the heck out of Bella, but we're mostly going to be indoors talking to Cindy, if she'll let us in. I'd like to look around the property, but I don't know if she'll permit that."

"Just tell me the time and place, and I'll be there."

Erin stopped by the police department after work, not knowing when the next time was that she'd be able to see

Terry. It was late enough that Clara Jones was gone for the day, but Melissa was there filing.

"Hi, Melissa. Is Terry in?"

"He's not, but he shouldn't be too far. Were you guys going to meet for supper?"

"No, I wanted to show him something. Police business."

"Oh." Melissa raised her brows curiously. "Really. Well, let me page him for you."

"I could just call his cell," Erin suggested.

"If it's police business, then I should page him. I don't get to do it very often! It always makes me feel... official!" Melissa gave Erin a wide smile and tossed her wildly curly hair.

"Oh, well... okay..."

Erin waited while Melissa sent the page from one of the computers. Melissa pressed the last key with a flourish.

"Like I said, he isn't far, so it shouldn't be very long."

Erin waited a little awkwardly. She hadn't thought about the possibility of Melissa being there; if she'd known, she would have picked a different day or time. But there wasn't much she could do about it. She was there, she couldn't exactly duck out and say she'd come back another time.

"So... you and Charley seem to have become fast friends," Erin commented, looking for a safe topic. "That's kind of cool."

Melissa's smile faltered. "I thought so at first," she said tentatively.

"Oh... things didn't turn out so well...?" Erin immediately felt guilty. She didn't have any control or influence over Charley, but she still felt responsible for Charley being in Bald Eagle Falls to begin with. If Charley had done something to hurt Melissa...

"She seemed like a lot of fun. I don't have a lot of close friends, even though I've always lived here. I thought... it was kind of like being in the popular clique at school all of a sudden. I should have known it would turn out to be a joke."

"She didn't... a joke? I'm really sorry, Melissa..."

"I don't mean... it wasn't like she was laughing and making fun of me. Not overtly. But I started to feel like... she was laughing behind my back. That it wasn't really me she was interested in, she just wanted to pump me for information about Davis."

Erin sighed. She had been afraid of that from the start. Charley was far too mercenary to be making friends with an older woman for no reason.

"I'm sorry she did that. I never said anything to her..."

"Of course not. I know you wouldn't be like that, Erin. But not everyone is like you, and I was... fooled at first."

It was about five minutes before Terry got there, K9 panting at his side. He smiled at Erin. "An official visit? What's up?"

Erin cleared her throat. "Could we go into your office?

Terry led the way and Melissa clucked in amusement, as if she thought it was just a ploy on Erin's part to get Terry alone. Terry motioned Erin ahead of him into the office, and stood with his hand on the door handle, his body language clearly asking whether he needed to shut it. Erin nodded. Terry shut it and went around his desk to sit behind it, treating it as an official interview.

"So...? This is all rather mysterious."

"I wasn't expecting Melissa to be here. It's just that it's about Davis, and you know..."

The rest went unsaid. That Melissa and Davis had recommenced their decades-old relationship and visited him at the prison. Terry needed to keep anything to do with Davis confidential from Melissa.

"Ah. Got it. So what do you have?" His expression was puzzled, not sure what else she could have come across about Davis.

"I've been reading Clementine's journal, you know."

"Sure."

"There is evidence that Davis knew about his brother's allergy."

"Well, we always suspected as much. What evidence?"

"He had a serious reaction. Davis took him to hospital. They told him it could have been fatal." Erin slid the book out of her shoulder bag and opened it to the marked page. Terry took his time reading through the passage a couple of times before looking up at Erin.

"You're right. They might be able to use this."

"Do you see… the margin marking and the smiley face?"

Terry nodded. "I wondered what that was about."

"That was Joelle. She marked a number of things in the journal."

"Really." Terry flipped back a few pages, noting other annotations. "Well, well, well. That made her smile, did it?" He pondered for a few minutes. "This could certainly be helpful to the case against Davis. Thanks for bringing it by. I'll make a copy and get it back to you."

Chapter Fourteen

ERIN'S FAMILIARITY WITH THE route to the Prost farm made it seem like it wasn't quite so far away as it was the first time. They were definitely out in the bush, but maybe it wasn't quite as remote as it had felt the first time. They pulled into the parking area, and Erin and Vic climbed out of the Challenger. A large black and white shaggy dog came streaking toward them, barking and growling so fiercely Erin was sure he was going to take a chunk out of her. She backed up into the side of the car, and fumbled behind her for the handle to get back in.

"Rasher, shut up!" a gruff voice shouted. "Go on, get out of here."

The dog lowered his head and looked back at the door of the farmhouse, where Cindy Prost stood with her hands on her hips. She pointed to the dog house.

"Go on. Back to your house. Leave the company alone."

He slunk obediently away and lay down in the dog house, head and front paws out the door.

Erin breathed heavily, holding one hand over her pounding heart. "Thank you. I guess we should have stayed in the car until after you came out. I didn't realize."

"It's a good practice if you're going to be visiting homes out in the bush. Most of us keep dogs to guard the house. Nobody is going to break into my house with Rasher in the yard."

"No," Erin agreed weakly. "I don't think so."

COUP DE GLACE

Cindy stood there for a moment gazing at them, hands on hips, then jerked her head.

"Come on in, then."

Erin walked up to the door. She was glad that Vic was there with her rather than Reg. Reg would enjoy getting this woman wound up, and that wasn't what Erin wanted. She would catch more flies with honey. Vic was far more sociable and wasn't likely to get them kicked off the property without what they had come for.

Bella was inside the house, hovering nearby, as if afraid she might get into trouble for acknowledging their presence. Cindy didn't say anything to Bella, neither telling her to leave nor encouraging her to stay.

"Come and set," Cindy invited, motioning to the living room. Vic and Erin found themselves seats. A good southern hostess, Cindy brought them tall glasses of iced tea and fiddled with the fans, trying to make sure they were pointed in Erin's and Vic's general direction. "I don't rightly understand why Bella wanted me to talk to you. This whole thing seems a little silly. If Bell wanted to know about my mother and father, she only needed to ask me."

"I have, Mom," Bella protested. "I've asked you about them lots of times, and you never want to tell me anything."

Cindy gave no sign that she heard a word her daughter was saying.

"I guess it's a bit of a local mystery," Erin said. "Family history can be so fascinating."

Cindy sat down in a carved rocking chair. She rocked back and forth a little, her movements slow. She took a sip of her tea and put it on the side table.

"It shorely is," she agreed. "I could tell you many stories about the history of the area. My family has lived here for hundreds of years. One of the first families to settle the area."

"That's what Bella was saying. What a long tradition. That's really amazing. I guess my family has been here for quite a while too, but I don't know all of the history and how our lines might intersect."

Cindy considered. "I don't rightly know. Been a long time since I pulled out those dusty old books. And..." Her eyes narrowed as she studied Erin and Vic in turn. "...I get the feeling that's not why you're here."

Erin shifted uncomfortably. She took a drink of her tea. "Uh... no. It's not really about my family. Or about ancient history. It was your parents I was curious about."

"And why?"

Erin tried to keep her eyes steady on Cindy and not let them drift over to Bella. "Like I said. A bit of local color. It sounded like an interesting story, and I was hoping you could fill me in on the details."

"You want to capitalize on our loss? Write a book about it or sell the story to the newspapers?"

"No. Nothing like that. I'm a baker. I'm not writing a book or articles for the paper. I just want to know what happened. Whatever you know, even if some of it is still a mystery today."

"This is Bella's doing. She put you up to it. I didn't like it when she took the job at the bakery. Told her she didn't need to be working while she was still going to school. She has everything she needs. Didn't need to be associating with..." her eyes shifted from Erin to Vic, "...odd people."

Vic gave a little snort at Cindy's pained expression. People like Lottie Sturm had already done their best to take Vic down a notch, to make her life miserable and drive her away. Cindy's distaste wasn't going to drive Vic to hysterical tears.

"Mom!" Bella said, red with embarrassment. "These are my bosses! You can't talk to them like that!"

"Because you might get fired? That's a risk that you faced by inviting them here. If they want to know what went on here, they're going to get the full Cindy Prost, undiluted."

"Just don't... call them names. Honestly!"

COUP DE GLACE

"I didn't call her *queer*," Cindy protested. "I said odd."

"That doesn't make a difference. Don't call them anything."

Cindy rolled her eyes and spread her hands in a 'what can you do about kids these days?' shrug at Erin and Vic. "Fine. So you came here to find out what happened to my mother. You think you're the only one who has ever asked?"

"No," Erin knew from Clementine's journal that more than one person had attempted to reason with Ezekiel Prost and to get him to allow them to search the grounds for any sign of Martha. But Ezekiel had denied them. If Cindy had been asked after she moved back to the farm, she suspected the inquirers didn't get much further with her. "I'm just hoping you'll share what you do know with us."

Cindy rocked. She had physical similarities to her daughter. Heavy. Blond hair—though Cindy's had a lot of gray in it. Her facial features were similar, though, of course, her skin was more wrinkled.

"Don't know what you think you're going to figure out that no one else has up until now. It's all pretty simple. My father told me that my mother was out every time I called to have a conversation. I started to wonder what was going on, whether she was ill and didn't want me to know about it, or maybe she'd even left him after some big blow-up. Some couples do that, you know, break up after all of the kids have moved out and they are on their own again."

Erin nodded. "Yes. It always bothers me when I hear about a couple that has been together for twenty-five or thirty years has broken up. It seems like such a waste."

Cindy made no response. Erin had the feeling that she was irritated by Erin's interruption to her carefully-considered narrative.

"So I was already wondering what was going on with my parents. Then I got a call from a friend."

From Lottie Sturm, as Clementine had suspected? Erin supposed it didn't make any difference who had called Cindy to tell her.

"She told me about how everyone was worried about Dad, and that Mom seemed to have disappeared. And just like that... my life changed forever."

Erin nodded. "So... you decided you'd better come home and see what was going on."

"You bet your sweet behind I did! Dropped everything, my whole life, and just came back out here."

"Did you find anything? Any sign of what had happened here?"

"Not a thing." Cindy shook her head. "You might think it's an exaggeration, but it's the truth. There was nothing to find. My mother wasn't here, but there was no indication she had planned to go on a long trip. I couldn't see any missing suitcase or clothes. All of her favorite things still seemed to be here. And no, there wasn't any sign that something violent had happened here, either. No bloody fingerprints. No rotting corpses. Just an old man..."

When Erin opened her mouth to ask about Ezekiel's age, Cindy talked over her.

"No, he wasn't that old in years. But it was like he was forty years older than he had been when I'd seen him the last Christmas. He had turned into an old man overnight. He wasn't eating, and his clothes just hung on him. He didn't say he was worried about my mom or that he was missing her, but he was obviously pining after her. Whyever she was gone... he was missing her something terrible. I think if I had taken another week to get here, he would have been dead."

Erin breathed out. "Wow. But you nursed him back to health. You took care of him, and he lived for a few more years."

COUP DE GLACE

Cindy ran her fingers through her hair. It wasn't curly, like Bella's. Bella had either inherited that from her father, or Cindy had outgrown her curls.

"My mother has been gone twenty-one years. Dad lived long enough to see his only grandchild, and she's seventeen now."

"Another four years." Not bad, for someone who had apparently been at death's door. But it was probably more than Cindy's cooking that had brought him back from the brink. It was Cindy herself. Family. Something to live for. Someone else to fill the empty spaces that his wife had left behind.

"That's really all there is to it. Nobody has ever found any trace of my mother, living or dead. I imagine sometimes that she's off enjoying life somewhere, that she started over and found the life that she couldn't have while she was living here and raising her children. But do I think she's off in Florida or Spain, enjoying the local color? Not really. I don't have proof of what happened, but I think she died."

Bella moved into the room to better hear or provide comfort. "Mom... is that what you really think? Why didn't you ever tell me?"

"I don't know how it happened. I hope he just woke up one morning and found that she had passed in the night. Or maybe she keeled over in the vegetable garden in the heat of the day. Just a natural occurrence. I don't like to think he might have done something to her."

"He wouldn't have," Bella said, as if she were the one who had known Grandpa and her mother the one who hadn't. "He wouldn't have done anything to hurt her, would he? He wasn't ever a violent person, right?"

Cindy didn't immediately jump in and say, 'Of course he wasn't. He'd never harmed a fly in his life. He'd never have laid a hand on his wife.' Instead, she pressed her lips together tightly, not answering for a few minutes.

"I don't know. When I was a kid, I was scared to death of him. He was bigger than life. If he told me to do anything and I questioned it, I'd get a whipping. There was never any doubt of that. But in the time I'd been away from home, he'd mellowed. He didn't have to be the authoritarian figure anymore. When I was little… I don't know if he ever struck my mother. I kind of assumed he did, but I never saw him do it. Maybe I just figured that if he whipped me, he must have hurt her too. My mother never said he did, but what woman would ever admit that to her child?"

"So it might have been violence. He might have killed her accidentally, or in a fit of anger," Vic suggested.

Cindy glared at her, clearly communicating that she was talking to Erin and didn't expect to hear any comments from Vic. She looked back at Erin and answered as if Erin had been the one to ask.

"I told you, there were no signs of violence. Nothing out of place. No blood. If he did hurt her… he cleaned everything up. He never said what he'd done. He never said my mother was dead."

"The townspeople assumed that he had done something to her. Or at the very least, that he'd disposed of the body."

"The townspeople have never had any idea about anything. Gossip and rumors. I've never had any reason to talk to anyone in the town about it."

"The Sheriff at the time? He never came out here?"

"He called me. Talked to me in town. I told him what I told you. There was no sign of anything on the farm. Nothing my father said ever convinced me that he had done anything to hurt her. She was just gone, and he was grieving for her."

"So the sheriff never came out?"

"He'd tried a couple of times before I came back. I made it clear to him that I would not be allowing anyone on the property either." Cindy picked up her glass and took a long drink, as if parched from her speech. "I never let anyone in here to talk about it, until now. The only reason I allowed you in was because you're Bella's boss."

"I really appreciate it," Erin said. "I know we don't have any right to just barge in here and demand details. You've been very gracious about it."

Cindy nodded her agreement. Erin didn't think she was only doing it for Bella. She had avoided Bella's questions in the past. Maybe she had just decided it was time to talk about it. Twenty years was a long time to stay quiet about something so life-changing. It had turned Cindy's life completely upside-down, putting her in the role of caregiver before she was prepared for it. Had Cindy ever considered abandoning her family property once her father was gone? Selling the farm that had been in her family for generations and going back to the city to work? It couldn't have been easy for her to eke out a living and to be isolated there for so much of the time. Just she and Bella.

"Would it be possible for us to look around the property a little?" Erin suggested, sure Cindy would say no.

But Cindy pursed her lips and considered. She rocked back and forth, and her eyes went over to Bella.

Bella leaned forward a little. "I could show them around, if you want. Then you wouldn't have to, but I'd make sure they didn't leave open any gates."

Cindy took another sip of tea. "All right," she agreed finally. "You can take them around. But stay away from the old barn. It isn't safe in there."

Bella nodded her understanding.

"We really appreciate it," Erin repeated. She swallowed and looked at Bella. "Do you want to show us around the house first?"

Again, she was sure that Cindy would jump in and snap at them, telling them they couldn't intrude on her family life. Looking outside at the goats was one thing. Poking through bedrooms was quite another. But Cindy just looked back at them, her eyes dark.

Bella managed to nod. "Sure, of course. We'll start upstairs."

There was a pause as everyone waited for an explosion, but one wasn't forthcoming. Had Cindy decided that she wanted them to look around? She wanted them to figure out the truth and expose it to the light of day twenty years later? It had been a burden that she had carried by herself for too long.

Erin and Vic stood up and followed Bella to the stairs. They all traipsed as quietly as possible up the squeaky risers. Bella hesitated for a moment, then indicated the first bedroom at the top of the stairs.

"I don't really know what you want to see. I mean… it's been years since Grandma and Grandpa lived here."

The first room appeared to be Cindy's room, the master bedroom. It was a small, cramped room, large enough for the bed and dresser, with patterned wallpaper that made Erin feel claustrophobic. She had lived in old houses, but none as old as the Prost farmhouse. What progenitor had originally erected those walls? Had it been one man? A family working together? A community project like a barn-raising? It was hot inside, which told Erin that it was not well-insulated and was probably freezing in the winter. Tennessee winters were nothing compared to the northeastern United States where Erin had spent most of her years, but they were still cold for someone with blood thinned by Tennessee summers. The closet was small by modern standards, but it had been built to hold all of a couple's clothes. Two pairs of pants, two shirts, and a good suit for the man. Two house dresses and a good dress for the woman. It wouldn't have accommodated much more.

"This is Mom's," Bella said unnecessarily. She looked around, as if seeing it with fresh eyes. "I guess when she moved back here, it must have been Grandma and Grandpa's."

Erin could see nothing that would give them any clues about Grandma's disappearance. What did they think, that the room would have been preserved as a shrine, still awaiting her return after twenty years? Cindy had moved on. She'd gone on to live her life.

Erin retreated to the hall and Bella took them on to the next room.

"Mine," Bella offered.

It was a typical teen girl's room. Vestiges of her childhood: dolls and middle grade books, posters of the current teen idols; an adult study desk, carefully arranged. Bella gave a shrug. "Mom's room when she was a girl. I guess she wanted me to have the same one as she had. Or to be in the room closest to her. I could pick one of the other ones if I wanted, but this is fine, and it's a pain to have to move everything."

Erin nodded. She didn't go in or spend long studying it. It wasn't like Grandma would have left a secret note for them to find, or Grandpa might have hidden a confession of guilt. It had been their daughter's room. Nobody was playing games.

There were two more bedrooms, one set up as a guest room and one holding excess furniture and other items they wanted to store. There was no upstairs bathroom.

"Was either of these used by your grandparents as a sewing room or study?" Erin asked.

Bella's shoulders lifted and fell. "Just bedrooms. I think they were both pretty outdoorsy, that's where they spent their time."

Erin nodded. "Okay. I don't think… I can't think of anything we need to see. We should look at the kitchen downstairs, but… I don't think we're going to find anything significant."

Bella took them back down the stairs. They nodded awkwardly at Cindy, who was still sitting in the rocker in the living room.

The kitchen was bright, with modern appliances that looked oddly out of place fit between old cupboards and counters. It was big enough for a small family to eat in. There wasn't a lot of space to store dishes or pantry items, but there was ample counter space for food preparation. No twenty-year-old blood spatters.

"And there's a cold room downstairs," Bella offered, but didn't indicate any desire to go down there herself.

"We should probably check that out," Erin said.

"No... there's nothing down there. Just shelves and canned goods."

Erin raised her eyebrows. "Then it will only take a minute to look. Where are the stairs?"

Bella reluctantly led them to the narrow door and opened it. She clicked on an electric light and stood to the side to allow Erin and Vic to go down.

"You're not coming?" Erin didn't really need to ask; the answer was obvious. Bella had no intention of venturing down to the basement. Maybe it wasn't haunted like she thought Auntie Clem's basement and the barn were, but it was still spooky enough that she wasn't going to go with them.

Erin led the way down the stairs. She tried not to let Bella's anxiety infect her. It was just a dug-out basement beneath an old house. There was nothing to worry about. No haints. No animals. Nothing that was any threat to them.

The lighting was dim, barely enough to see by. The stairs were bare wood, as was the handrail mounted on the wall beside them. It was much cooler than the rest of the house, enough to make Erin shiver. There had been some attempt made to put up wallboard and a subfloor, but it was clumsy and haphazard and didn't do much to enhance the space. Erin walked out into the middle of the cold room and gazed around at the jars of home-canned fruit together with commercial cans of vegetables and other products. There were some large sacks of grains and other dry goods, and the distinctive smell of rotting potatoes. Vic and Erin looked around at their surroundings and then each other.

"Could have buried her under the floor," Vic said, tapping the wood floor with her toe. It was still yellow rather than the gray that older wood turned. Of fairly recent vintage.

Erin nodded. "I don't smell anything dead."

"You wouldn't after twenty years."

"No, I guess not."

Erin looked at the floor, seeing whether there was a way to lift some of the floorboards up to have a peek underneath, but everything seemed to be nailed down securely. The floor had been laid before the walls, so it disappeared under the wallboard rather than ending before it.

"Nothing else to see," Vic said.

"Okay. Back up."

They both tried to look as if they were not hurrying for the stairs, and there wasn't exactly a scuffle at the bottom to see who would go first, but there was definitely a moment of awkwardness as they shifted and tried to decide who would go first. Erin had led the way down, so she figured it was her right to be the first one up and, in the end, she got the first position, walking back up into the oppressive heat of the day.

"I told you there wasn't anything," Bella said.

"And now we checked, so we know," Vic agreed.

"So you want to see the rest of the farm?" Bella led them out of the house.

Chapter Fifteen

STEPPING OUT INTO THE sun, Erin immediately regretted the choice to search the Prost property in the heat of the afternoon. They should have been there in the early morning as soon as the sun came up, or the evening as it went down, not right in the middle of it. She couldn't imagine how they were going to traipse all over the farm without fainting of heat and dehydration. Erin put her sunglasses on, but she needed a hat. And an air-conditioned car.

Bella led them to the parking area and pointed to a small vehicle that seemed to be a cross between an ATV and a jeep. "Climb on."

Vic didn't hesitate; in fact, she seemed eager to climb aboard. Erin was the only one who seemed to have reservations about the idea. She stood looking at the dirty, chipped, open-air vehicle.

"Uh… you drive?" she asked Bella.

"Sure, I've been driving this thing around for years. Trust me, you don't want to have to walk."

Erin reluctantly climbed into the vehicle. "Is this safe? There are no seatbelts."

"If it rolled over, you'd be pinned underneath," Bella said blithely, "so no seatbelts."

Erin looked at Vic. "If it rolled over?"

"Don't think about it. Bella knows what she's doing. Enjoy it!"

COUP DE GLACE

Erin hung on to whatever she could reach, thinking more about how to remain in the vehicle than of enjoying the ride. Bella keyed the ignition and the engine roared to life. Clouds of exhaust billowed out behind them. Before Erin had the chance to prepare herself, Bella put the car into gear and they started moving.

They bounced over the uneven ground. Erin felt every bump and clung tightly to her handholds. Vic give a whoop and leaned forward, looking like she was having the time of her life. She and Bella shouted to each other over the roar of the engine, but Erin couldn't hear most of what they were saying. She was supposed to be paying attention to the landscape, looking for any clues as to what might have happened to Bella's grandma. It wasn't like she would find disturbed earth or new growth where a fresh grave had been dug; Mother Nature would have reclaimed the area over the ensuing decades. She tried to force herself to pay attention to the passing landscape anyway and strained to hear Bella's comments as she gestured to various areas.

The road, if it could be called that, was rough and rutted, just a trail worn through the ground cover. They broke free of the thick growth of trees into a clearing, and Erin shaded her eyes from the sun in spite of her sunglasses. Bella pulled the car over to the side and parked it. The engine quieted a little.

"This is the lower pasture," Bella explained, motioning to the goats grazing or resting in the field. It wasn't flat like a farmer's field. It was hilly and rough and the pasture itself was on a fairly steep slope. But Erin knew that goats could climb just about anything. They looked tranquil and happy in the pasture and paid no attention at all to the roar of the engine intruding on their peaceful munching.

Erin evaluated it and found nothing unusual or out of place. "This is the same pasture as your grandma would have used?"

"Sure. Same one as has been here forever."

"And goats aren't like pigs, they won't eat just anything, right?"

Vic looked at Erin questioningly. Bella shook her head. "Goats will eat all kinds of things, food or not. You have to make sure there's no poisonous plants or anything else that might harm them in the field."

"But they're herbivorous. Not omnivorous, like pigs."

"Yeah." Bella gave a little shrug, her mind not following the same tracks as Erin's.

But Vic's face showed that she knew exactly what Erin was thinking. Pigs had been used by more than one serial killer to dispose of human bodies. She wrinkled her nose and shook her head at Erin. Erin gazed at the goats in the field.

"And you've always had goats? Not any other animal?"

"Goats are the best," Bella said. "In these parts, there isn't lots of flat land and it takes time and effort to clear the trees. You can't grow wheat here. Cows don't do well here. But goats do. That's what we've been raising for generations."

Erin nodded. "Is there anything else to see?"

Bella put the car back into gear, and they bounced around some more, winding around through the trees. They stopped at a large, curve-roofed metal structure. "This is the barn. The goat barn. This is where they come to shelter at night."

"How long has this been here?"

"I dunno. Thirty, forty years."

"So it was here when your grandma disappeared."

"Yeah, I guess so. Not much has changed since then. Everything is done pretty much the same."

"And the red barn was never used for goats? The one that—"

Bella waved away the rest of the question. "No. Back when they had horses, that's probably where they were kept. Maybe a milk cow. Garden stuff. Farming equipment."

"And it hasn't been used since your grandma... disappeared?"

"No. Mom had a horse when she was a little girl, but it died... maybe when she was a teenager, I'm not sure when. I think that was the last horse they had. And I don't know when they had a cow last. Mom doesn't talk about having to milk cows, so I don't think they had one when she lived here."

"Should we go in?"

Bella raised her eyebrows. "Do you want to? Not much to see."

"I'd like to, if we're allowed."

"Mom said to stay out of the old barn, she didn't say we couldn't come to this one." Bella shut off the car engine, and Erin and Vic followed her to the barn.

Even before they stepped inside, Erin was regretting the request. The pungent smell of goat filled her nostrils, making her nauseated. She breathed as shallowly as she could, through her mouth, but she could still smell and almost taste the rank, muddy smell of the goats. They weren't as bad as pigs. Erin remembered going to a farm on a field trip when she was younger. The pig pens had been so revolting, she had thrown up her lunch, causing chaos among her classmates. She was glad she hadn't stayed too long in that family. She had endured all kinds of teasing at school, and introductions always included 'the one who threw up on the farm trip.'

"Are you okay?" Vic asked.

Erin swallowed and nodded. "It's just... the smell."

"Takes some getting used to," Bella admitted. "I've been around them all my life, and it still bothers me when the wind is blowing from the west."

But she didn't seem to have any problem marching up to the building and throwing a door open. She groped for a switch in the darkness inside the door and turned on some lights. Erin held her breath and stood in the doorway for a quick look around, then backed out again to breathe. Vic went into the barn and took a few minutes before coming out. She made no comment on Erin's swift departure and spoke in a low voice before Bella finished up and joined them.

"The floors are slatted so that waste flows down into pits under the building. I don't know what the procedure is for getting them flushed or mucked out, but I assume they've been cleaned at least annually since Grandma disappeared. If there were any remains down there, I doubt if anyone could find them now."

Erin nodded. Bella exited the barn, shutting the lights back off and pulling the door shut. She didn't, Erin noted, lock the door. Why would they need to? It was out in the middle of nowhere, and why would anyone want to break into a goat barn? If they did, what harm could they do?

They all walked back to the vehicle. Bella seemed happy to be outdoors, unaware of the grisly conversation Erin and Vic were having. They all climbed into the car and proceeded on to another field, this one without any goats, that Bella said was the upper pasture. Erin could see that the growth there was longer, with leggy weeds and hardy grasses. Presumably, when the lower pasture got too short, the goats would be moved to the upper pasture.

Erin couldn't think of anything to ask. She nodded and looked around. Off to the right, she could see white posts and dark shapes. "What's that?"

"Family graveyard," Bella said. "You want to see?"

"Yes."

Bella put the car in gear and took them in a curving route to a little cemetery in a glade. The posts Erin had been able to see had been crosses, and the dark shapes various statues and monuments. Erin was first out of the car, and the others followed her. Erin explored the cemetery, fascinated. She'd rarely been to a regular cemetery before, and never to a family cemetery. She walked from one grave to the other, looking at the family names, the husbands and wives buried side by side. The tragic little gravestones with cherubs for babies who had died in infancy. Most of the marker stones were modest, but there were a few big ones with statues that towered over the others. Erin heard approaching footsteps, and Bella came up beside her. They browsed over the stones, Bella pointing out a few relatives or telling what she knew about this person or that. They made their way down an aisle, and Bella pointed.

"Over there, that's Grandpa's grave."

Erin approached it and looked down at the stone. Black with gray engraving. Just Ezekiel's name and the dates of his birth and death. No scripture, no 'loving father and husband,' no angel motif. Erin studied it.

"You said your mom is Christian?"

Bella nodded. "Yeah. We don't go to church every week, but she's still Christian."

Erin nodded thoughtfully. Maybe Cindy hadn't told them everything she knew about Ezekiel and what had happened to Martha.

"It's been a long time since I've been here," Bella mused, gazing around. "It looks different. I guess it's just because of growing up. Everything from your childhood seems smaller than you remember."

Erin withdrew her focus from the one gravestone to again take in the neat rows and columns of the plots. Somebody kept it maintained. Not the golf-short grass of a city cemetery, but it wasn't overgrown either. Some of the plots, like one of the ones next to Ezekiel, didn't have markers. Maybe they'd had wooden markers that had rotted away, or maybe there had never been markers, but slight depressions in the ground showed where the ground had settled in the graves.

"It's a beautiful little place," Erin said. "Maybe it's a weird thing to say, but I love it. I've never been in a cemetery like this before."

Bella beamed. "I like it too. Even though there are lots of bodies buried here, I've never felt like it was haunted. It's not spooky." She shrugged. "I guess that's because it's consecrated ground."

Erin nodded. She wasn't sure exactly what that meant, but it probably wasn't the time to ask.

With Bella beside her and Vic somewhere behind looking at other gravestones, Erin was startled by a movement in the trees ahead of them.

"Who's over there?" a man's voice demanded.

Chapter Sixteen

BELLA DIDN'T SEEM PERTURBED to be addressed in such a way out in the middle of the bush. She peered through the trees.

"It's me, Mr. Ware. Bella Prost."

"Bella?" the man's voice repeated.

Erin watched him emerge slowly from the cover of the trees. An old man, solidly built and slow moving, each step deliberate. Erin tried to estimate his age. Sixty? Seventy? His hair was gray, his face deeply wrinkled by many years in the sun. It took a few minutes for him to make his way over to them.

"Erin, this is Mr. Ware," Bella introduced. "He lives the next property over. The boundary line is just over there. You see the fence posts…?"

Erin squinted at the trees Mr. Ware had come through. She could just barely see the fence posts. The wire in between them was invisible from where they stood. Apparently, there was a break or a gate somewhere that Mr. Ware had come through. It wasn't an old, weathered fence like Erin expected to see, but something newer that had been erected in the last five or ten years. The posts were too white to be wood, but were maybe some kind of plastic or other synthetic.

"It's nice to meet you, Mr. Ware."

"Erin is my boss," Bella told him. "She's the owner and head baker over at Auntie Clem's Bakery."

"At the bakery? I thought the bakery closed."

"The Bake Shoppe closed, this is a new one. Erin opened it where the tea room used to be."

"You run the tea room?" Mr. Ware asked Erin, apparently either hard of hearing or deliberately misunderstanding.

"I have a bakery where the tea room used to be," Erin said in a loud, firm voice. "You should come by sometime and have a look."

Mr. Ware barely glanced at Erin, looking instead at Bella for clarification. "Is that the new-fangled place?" he asked. "I hear they have all kinds of inedible, weird stuff there."

Bella's face was flushing red. "Mr. Ware! I've told you about the bakery before. Erin bakes great bread, and all kinds of treats too!"

There was a twinkle in Mr. Ware's eye that gave him away. Erin shook her head. "You're a tease, Mr. Ware. Don't think I don't see you for what you are."

Just a hint of a smile peeked through Mr. Ware's craggy face. "Who, me?"

Bella gave him a playful punch in the arm, just skimming his sleeve. "You're so bad! I never know when you're being serious."

"I've dealt with people like this before," Erin said gravely. "There's a trick to it."

Both Bella and Mr. Ware looked at her expectantly. Erin could hear Vic somewhere close behind her as well. She leaned toward Bella slightly, and said in a low voice. "You don't believe a word that comes out of his mouth."

Bella laughed, and Mr. Ware chuckled appreciatively. He put a hand over his heart.

"You've wounded me, young lady! Wounded me deeply."

Erin cocked her head, looking at him. "How long have you lived here?" she asked. "I assume this is your family farm?"

COUP DE GLACE

Mr. Ware made a little wave to the land behind him. "This has been Ware land for a long time," he agreed. "I was born here, lived here my whole lifetime."

"Then you must have known Ezekiel and Martha."

He stilled. The twinkle had disappeared from his eye. Together, the three of them looked down at Ezekiel's marker.

"Yes, I knew Ezekiel and Martha," he admitted. "Tragic how we lost them both. But you live out here long enough, and you learn that sooner or later, everyone departs this earth at some point. Some earlier, some later, but eventually, everyone."

"That's true," Erin agreed. "My mom and dad were both gone years ago. But what do you mean about the way we lost Ezekiel and Martha? I thought nobody knew what happened to Martha, and didn't Ezekiel just die of natural causes?"

Mr. Ware scratched his chin, considering his answer. "Everyone in these parts figured that Ezekiel knew what happened to Martha, even though he would never say. A woman just doesn't up and leave after thirty years of marriage without any warning. She didn't drive. No one picked her up. So where did she go? No, I'm afeared that something happened between her and Ezekiel." Mr. Ware stared down at the headstone. "I'm not saying what. The only one who knows for sure is Ezekiel and the good Lord, and Ezekiel's been gone these sixteen, seventeen years. He took that secret with him. We won't know until the hereafter."

"But you think Ezekiel had something to do with it? He had a fight with her...?"

"Everybody knew the two of them had their problems. But somehow, she disappeared. A lady who doesn't drive just doesn't up and disappear without someone helping her along."

"No," Erin agreed. She hoped to hear something more concrete from Mr. Ware, one of the only remaining witnesses as to what might have happened. But it sounded like it was just the same rumors as she'd heard elsewhere. "Martha never said anything to you? That she was planning on leaving her husband? That he had hurt or threatened her? That things weren't good between them?"

"I wouldn't want to speak ill of the dead. I can't say she ever said anything like that to me. But he wasn't an easy man to get along with."

Erin was going to repeat what Cindy had said about Ezekiel being abusive, but Bella might not want this repeated to someone else. She glanced over at Bella and decided against it.

"But you don't know. What happened to Martha, I mean."

Mr. Ware shook his head slowly. "I can't be certain he did something to her. But I don't see what other explanation there is."

"She might have died naturally, or accidentally, and he just... didn't report it."

"But why wouldn't he? Only if he had something to do with it and didn't want anyone else to know."

Erin sighed. "Maybe."

He stared at her closely for a moment, then looked over at Bella. "Why are you asking these questions? You're not part of this family. You're not even from these parts. Why do you care?"

"Erin is helping me," Bella said. "I always wanted to know the real story, and she's helping me out. And she is from here. Clementine Price was her aunt. She lived here."

Erin was going to correct her, as they hadn't actually lived in Bald Eagle Falls, but had only stayed there temporarily. But Bella wasn't intentionally misleading him, and it was probably better if he thought she was a native.

COUP DE GLACE

"You shouldn't go digging up the past," Mr. Ware said. "Just let things be."

"We just want to know the truth," Erin said. She didn't tell him that Bella wanted to know so that Martha would stop haunting the barn. That might be a bit too much honesty.

"You should just leave it alone," Mr. Ware repeated. "What's going to change even if you did find out what really happened? It isn't going to make any difference to anyone, it will just smear Ezekiel's good name."

"Since everybody thinks Ezekiel killed her, I'm not exactly smearing anyone's name. Maybe we could even clear him. Maybe he had nothing to do with her disappearance."

Erin wasn't sure how she could prove this. So far, she wasn't having much luck with finding anything out.

Erin had spent the evening in the bakery kitchen with Vic, blending up a number of sweet concoctions and pouring them into molds. Thursday morning, she would have the cold case at the bakery filled with frozen treats. She was excited to see how the kids—and the adults—enjoyed eating dairy-free ice creams and gourmet popsicles to beat the heat. The days were getting warmer and warmer, and during the days while she had sweated by the sweltering ovens, she had dreamed up the most delicious frozen concoctions she could think of to cool off with in the coming months. Not just frozen lemonade and watermelon, but dairy-free chocolate caramel ice cream sandwiched between two gluten-free vanilla cookies, sunflower butter pies in chocolate shells, popsicles with colorful layers of blended berries and fruits, and traditional dipped banana pops.

It was extra work to be preparing frozen treats on top of the usual baking, but she figured that once they took off, she could cut down on some of the hot baking in the morning as people chose frozen treats in place of their usual cookies and cakes.

"You know, I think the orange creamsicles are going to be my favorite," Vic offered, as she took another batch of molds to the freezer. "I know they're not anything fancy or new, but sometimes the traditional foods have stayed around for a reason."

"I'm not going to diss the orange creamsicles," Erin agreed. "They're lovely."

"You really know your stuff, Erin. These things are going to sell like hotcakes—or coldcakes!"

"I hope so."

There was a knock at the back door, and after a moment the door opened, and Erin turned to see Terry looking in.

"Let yourself in," she called. "We just have our hands full right now."

He entered with K9 and shut the door behind him. In the kitchen, he looked around at the counters full of fruits and various concoctions.

"Working on your cold case, I see."

Erin looked sideways at him. "Yup."

"And how is the other cold case going?"

"Not really going much of anywhere, as far as I can tell. Everywhere I go, they pretty much just confirm what I heard in the beginning. Grandma Prost disappeared, everybody assumed Grandpa killed her or found her dead and took care of the body, but no one could find anything out for sure. I think interest died out when Cindy got home and didn't have news about finding her mother's decomposing body in the bed."

"Your partner in crime seems to think there's been progress in the case."

Erin looked over at Vic, puzzled.

"Not Vic, your sister."

"Oh." Erin's stomach turned queasily. "Reg."

COUP DE GLACE

"She's spreading talk around town about the ghost of Grandma Prost demanding justice, wanting to know why her killer was never pursued and prosecuted."

Although Reg was still staying with Erin, things had been quiet the last couple of days and she had hoped that Reg was losing interest in Bald Eagle Falls and Bella's grandma.

"I didn't know that. She hasn't said anything to me about it."

"That's a little difficult to believe."

Vic looked at Terry. "Erin hasn't been encouraging Reg. Right from the start, she's been trying to get Reg to just move on."

"By inviting her to stay here and taking her to the Prost farm."

"I didn't invite her here," Erin protested. "She invited herself. I couldn't leave her out on the street with nowhere to live. She's supposed to be finding a place of her own to rent. And I didn't take her to Bella's. She could have gone in her own car; Bella invited her over. I went to keep an eye on things and make sure it didn't go too far."

"It's gone too far."

"Okay. I'll talk to her. Or at least, I'll try to talk to her. I don't know how much good it will do."

"Is she here?"

Erin shook her head. "No. I think she's gone into the city, but she didn't tell me where she was going or what her plans were. She doesn't keep a baker's schedule, so our paths don't cross much, unless she has something she wants to talk to me about."

Terry considered for a moment, then nodded and pulled out one of the kitchen chairs and sat down. Erin recognized this as a signal that he was done interrogating her and was ready to step out of his law enforcement role and relax.

"It's hard to believe that the two of you came from the same family. Reg is so different from you."

"I hope so. And we're not from the same family. We both came from other families, and then had several foster families. Just because we shared one foster home, that doesn't mean we were raised together. We only lived together for a few months. Not even a year."

"She calls herself your sister."

"Reg says a lot of things. You need to take anything that comes out of her mouth with a grain of salt."

"She's quite the con artist, isn't she?"

Erin nodded slowly. "Yes… if you want to call it that."

"What would you call it?"

Erin considered. "She's… creative. She always has a new scheme for making some money. Not necessarily anything illegal, but sometimes it crosses the line."

Terry raised one eyebrow. "And how often were you involved in these… schemes?"

"She was older than I was. She would involve me with things… use me as a scapegoat if we got caught. She figured I wouldn't get in as much trouble as she would."

"Sounds like a sibling."

Erin took a deep breath, determined to make a clean breast of it. "When we had both aged out, she kept in touch, and she pulled me into a few other schemes, before I thought better of it and told her I wouldn't do anything else with her."

"When you were old enough to know better."

"Does an eighteen-year-old have that much more sense than a fifteen-year-old? I don't know. Figuring everything out at that age is hard. I had to support myself and Reg had ideas of how to do that. I wanted it to be easy."

"But making a living isn't easy. There are no easy answers."

"That's what I eventually figured out. I'm not sure if Reg ever will."

COUP DE GLACE

"What is her background? Why hasn't she learned that?"

Erin grimaced, trying to figure out what to tell Terry. "Her history is her own business. We learned in foster care that people's pasts and families are their own. Reg has a right to her privacy."

"The citizens of Bald Eagle Falls have their rights too. Don't you think they have the right to know her history?"

"Not really," Erin said honestly. "They should be able to see what she is and judge for themselves. *You* could see what she was up to."

"And I have access to databases where I can see what kind of record she has. Regular citizens don't have that."

Erin scraped out the contents of one of the blenders, and half-filled a cup, which she set in front of Terry.

"If people are looking for a medium, they want to be deceived. If they want to pay to be deceived, then they get what they pay for."

"I can see how you would adopt that position, because you're an atheist and you don't believe in spirits and mediums. But people around here do. So that's what they are paying for. They think they really are getting someone who can talk to spirits."

"Like I say, they want to be deceived."

Terry scowled, looking for a way to better express his position.

"I don't think you're going to talk Erin out of it," Vic said. "You have to believe in spirits to think that people are paying for something other than a show."

"I suppose," Terry grumbled. He took a sip of the smoothie Erin had given him. "Mm. This is good. What is it?"

"Watermelon raspberry."

"Very nice."

"Thanks. And I am sorry about Reg. I didn't ask her here or plan on her following me here. It's one of the hazards of using my real name."

Terry looked as if this aspect had never occurred to him before. "Is that why you assumed other names?"

Erin hesitated. "Well, it's one of them," she admitted.

Terry studied her as he had another sip of his watermelon raspberry smoothie.

When Erin got home from the bakery, Reg was just getting home as well. Her cheeks were pink and her dark eyes sparkling, signs that she was pleased with herself. When she saw Erin, she lowered her eyes, trying to suppress her mood.

"Oh, hey, Erin. How was your day?"

Erin nodded. "Okay. Busy, as usual. You're looking happy. You find an apartment?"

That threw cold water over Reg's mood. She attempted to school her expression, but couldn't keep her smile from faltering.

"Uh, no. Still looking."

"So what's up?" Erin let herself into the house and Reg followed.

"Just making contacts... networking..." Reg said vaguely.

"Officer Piper was around today. He said you're causing problems."

"Problems?" Reg raised her brows, affecting an innocent expression. "I don't know what he could mean."

"He said you're spreading rumors around and stirring things up."

"Do you expect me to not talk about my business? I made contact with Martha Prost; that's news. That's something that people want to hear about. Maybe they have relatives they want to get in touch with."

COUP DE GLACE

"You shouldn't be capitalizing on someone else's loss." Erin lowered her voice to a confidential tone, even though there was no one there to overhear them. "You really upset Bella, you know. You were supposed to be reassuring her, not getting her more upset. She's been quite troubled about the idea of her grandma being cold somewhere and not being laid to rest with her husband."

Reg shrugged. She slipped off a heavy shoulder bag and sat it on one of the kitchen chairs. "It isn't my fault that her grandma isn't buried there. I can't help it if she finds that upsetting."

"You're the one who suggested it was a problem."

"She wanted to know why her grandma's spirit wasn't at rest." Reg lifted her hands, palms up in offering. "Well, there you are. The reason she isn't able to rest."

"But it isn't something that Bella or Cindy can do anything about."

"That's not my problem."

Erin blew out her breath in frustration. "You were just trying to leave things open so that she'd ask you back again."

Reg put a hand dramatically over her heart as if wounded. "Erin! You think I'm trying to take advantage of your friend?"

"Yes! Exactly!"

Reg laughed and had the grace not to deny it.

"I don't think you realize how what you're doing can affect people's lives," Erin said. "You have the opportunity to make people feel better, but instead, you're making them worse. You don't know if someone might be really depressed. You might be pushing someone over the edge."

"You sound like your friend Adele." Reg rolled her eyes dramatically. "'You don't know the powers you're dealing with.' Please. I don't have any special power or influence. People are going to believe what they want to believe. Bella wants to believe her grandma's spirit is restless, because she feels disconnected. She wants to pretend to be doing something." Reg gave a shrug. "I'm just a mirror, reflecting back what she wants to see."

"If you keep spreading around town what happened at the farm the other day, it's going to get back to Cindy. You'll get Bella in trouble with her."

"It was Bella's choice to invite us and Bella's choice to do it behind her mother's back. She's the one who set it up that way, not me."

"You need to stop talking about it."

"I didn't sign a nondisclosure agreement. This is my business. Word of mouth is the best advertising."

Erin shook her head, clenching her teeth together to keep herself from saying anything that might cross the line. She wasn't responsible for Reg Rawlins. She couldn't control what Reg did. If people judged her as being part of what Reg was doing, that was their problem. They should know Erin better.

"Did you ever apologize to Adele?"

"Apologize for what?"

"You said you would apologize for being rude to her."

Reg waved the issue away. She probably didn't even remember what she had promised. She wasn't one to get all in a knot over keeping promises or what someone else thought was right. She never intended to do what she had said, she had just wanted Erin off her back. "I haven't seen her around. She must not spend very much time in town. I'll tell her next time I see her."

"You were rude to her. You said you'd apologize."

"I just said I would. What do you want me to do? Go to her house?"

Adele's house was her sanctuary. Erin didn't know if Adele would ever forgive her if she sent Reg over there. And if Erin pushed it too much, Reg might start spreading rumors about Adele. Adele had a tenuous reputation as it was. If the townspeople decided she was more witch than wise woman, she could get run out of town, just as she had been run out of other communities.

"Just… tone it down a little," Erin suggested. "If you don't want to get into trouble, you should be trying to keep a low profile."

She should have known that telling Reg not to do something would not go over well. Erin herself had the same failing. Telling her what to do always stirred up feelings of rebellion. No longer a teenager, Erin tried to control those inclinations, but Reg was different. Erin needed to appeal to Reg's self-interests rather than urging the 'right' course.

"Terry's suspicions are already up," Erin persisted. "I'd hate to see him arrest you on some trumped-up charge because you're disturbing the usual balance of things here."

Reg considered this. "Yeah, okay." She nodded. "I appreciate the heads-up."

Chapter Seventeen

THE HEAT OF THE afternoon brought even more customers than usual, as word of Erin's frozen creations spread through town. Mothers brought their young children in, towing them back out into the fresh air with flushed faces and popsicle smiles.

Then the older children started to arrive as they were let out of school. Erin did a brisk trade, accepting pocket change and distributing the ice cream, frozen lemonade, and other cold desserts.

Erin recognized one of the childish voices and looked over the customers to pick out young Peter Foster, one of her favorite customers. He introduced his friends to the bakery, telling them about Erin's delicious baked goods. Some of the other children had eaten her food before, their mothers picking up bakery items or at the Halloween party Vic and Erin had thrown in Erin's back yard. They did everything they could to introduce new customers to the delicious gluten-free baking, proving that it really could be just as good as its gluten-filled counterparts. It didn't have to taste like cardboard or have the texture of sand.

"Hello, Peter," Erin called over to him. "How was school today?"

Peter gave her a brilliant smile. "Hi, Miss Erin! We came for popsicles."

"You're not the only ones. What would you like?"

"I don't know. Everything sounds so good! What's your favorite?"

COUP DE GLACE

"Hmm…" Erin considered the available selection. "I really like the cherries jubilee frozen lemonade. If you like sweet and tart. If you like something richer… the chocolate cheesecake frozen cones."

Peter considered, and discussed those and other options with his friends. Just like when Peter came in with his mother and sisters, he encouraged his friends to all pick something different, so everyone could share a bite of each different treat. He finally went with the chocolate cheesecake cone, his little friends made their selections, and all of the money was pooled together.

"Okay, you're all paid up," Erin told them. "Enjoy!"

They had all grabbed their selections from the cold case, so they headed outside to sit in the benches outside the bakery's front door, shaded by the colorful awnings that stretched away from the buildings, to visit with each other and enjoy their purchases.

Erin looked at her watch again, frowning. She understood that sometimes employees were going to be late or absent. They were held up at a traffic accident. They got up in the morning with a sore throat. Something unexpected happened.

But Bella or any other good employee should know to pick up the phone and give Erin a call to let her know what was going on. It was common sense.

But it was opening time and Bella wasn't there. She hadn't shown up for the prep. She hadn't called to say that she'd slept in but would be there for the start of business. Erin flipped the sign on the door to open and went back behind the counter to serve customers. The first few customers trickled in, some of them yawning, some of them bright-eyed. It was amazing how differently people's bodies handled the early morning.

She was too busy to think of much else as she tried to greet people, help them with their choices, and then ring them up at the till.

Erin was surprised when Terry walked into the bakery during the busy time. He knew the general ebb and flow of customers at Auntie Clem's and usually timed his visits for when it was quiet, and Erin would be able to chat. The second surprise was that he walked around the lineup of customers waiting for their turns, barging in front of the queue.

"Terry? Is something wrong?"

"Is Bella here?"

"No, she didn't show up for work today."

"She was scheduled, though?"

"Yes."

"Did she call you? Explain why she wouldn't be here?"

Erin put her hands on the counter, bracing herself. "No. What's going on, Terry? You're scaring me."

"She's missing."

"Missing?"

"Her mother called the police department this morning."

"But… what happened? Did Cindy wake up in the morning and Bella was gone? Did she go out and not come back? What?"

"She was apparently supposed to go out and put the goats to pasture. When she hadn't returned, Cindy went looking for her. The vehicle Bella should have been using was in the driveway, but she was nowhere to be found."

"Had Bella left and returned, or not gone out?"

"The goats were in the pasture."

"So she had done it and come back."

"Except there was no sign she'd come back, other than the vehicle. I'm going out there to help search for her. But we're pretty confused as to what might have happened."

COUP DE GLACE

"I didn't hear anything from her this morning. I thought... she'd slept in... I was pretty angry she hadn't even called." Erin felt sick to her stomach with guilt and worry.

"You couldn't have known there was anything wrong."

"Where are you going to search for her?"

"We'll start with the farm. That's the last place she was seen and where she should be. All of the Prost vehicles are there."

"What can I do?"

Terry turned his head to look at the customers waiting in line. "I think you've got your hands full at the moment. We'll get started and I'll let you know what we find."

Erin breathed out. "Okay. Thanks. Did you let Vic know?"

"I'm going to see if she can pin down Willie for me. He would be helpful out at the farm."

"Yeah. For sure. He's always willing to help; it's just a matter of finding out where he is and if he can get over there. He likes Bella, I'm sure he'll want to be part of the search team."

Erin didn't want to tell Terry goodbye; once he was gone it would really sink in that something was wrong, and Bella wasn't just going to show up late with an apology. Erin felt like if she could keep Terry from leaving, it wouldn't really be happening. That was silly, and she should let him get out of there as soon as possible so that he could find out what had happened to Bella.

"Did Cindy check the barn? I know Bella's not supposed to go in there, but maybe she did...?"

"I'll check when I get there. When you were out there, there wasn't anywhere else that made you uneasy? Maybe something Bella said she would check later?"

"No." Erin closed her eyes, trying to marshal her thoughts and put all of the memories in order so she could pull out anything important or unusual. "We toured around the farm... everything in the house seemed perfectly normal. The barn was rundown and gross, but I don't think there was really anything dangerous there. Certainly not Grandma Prost's ghost. There was..."

"What?" Terry prompted impatiently, when Erin couldn't quite catch the fleeting thought.

"When we looked at the goat barn—well, Vic went in, I couldn't get past the door—but we were looking for places that a body might had been disposed of and never found—and Vic was talking about the waste pit under the barn. She was talking about how deep it was..."

Terry gave a small shudder. "Well, that won't be a fun job. I hope we don't have to dredge it out."

"No one would have put Bella down there. Tell me no one would be sick enough to do something like that. Bella's our friend. She's only seventeen."

"Assuming that Bella's disappearance is not a coincidence... what's the difference between murdering an old woman and a teenage girl? If you can kill with cold disregard for human life... age really doesn't have anything to do with it. Whoever did this—if they are related—has already proven to be cold and cunning."

Realization washed over Erin. She hadn't actually equated the disappearance of Bella with the disappearance of her grandmother.

"If someone took Bella because of our investigation into her grandma..."

"It's not your fault, Erin. It's the fault of whoever did it. If anyone. There might be a perfectly innocent reason she didn't go back to the house, and she's still somewhere on the farm, unharmed..."

"But if someone took her..."

"What?"

"That means it wasn't Grandpa Prost. Right from the start, everyone assumed he knew where Martha was, and he had done something to her. But if Bella's disappearance is related, that means Grandpa Prost didn't do it. We've been looking at the wrong person for twenty years."

Erin felt like she was in a daze for the rest of the work day, trying to stay focused on her customers and their needs, but continually trying to take in the fact that Bella was missing and that she might hold a key to what had happened. Vic showed up an hour or so after Terry's visit, advising that she and Willie had cut their day off short and Vic figured Erin could use the help while Willie went to the farm to help Terry.

"I can't believe any of this," Vic said. "We were just there. Everything seemed so… innocuous. Whatever happened to Martha Prost, it was twenty years ago. Why would anyone care about it now?"

Erin counted out the cookies she was packing three times before she was sure she had it right.

"There's no statute of limitations on murder. If they thought that they were going to be discovered, they might have panicked."

"And kidnapped Bella? How is that going to make things any better?"

"If Bella knew something."

"But you and I know she didn't."

"Somebody thought she did."

Vic pressed her fingertips to her temples, massaging them briefly. "I just don't get it. What could she have said to tip anyone off?"

"I think pretty much everyone in town knew we were looking at the death again. Even if you and I and Bella kept it quiet, Reg has been spouting off about it all over the place."

"Reg! Where is she? Has anyone talked to her about this?"

Erin looked over at Vic. "Why would anyone talk to her?"

"To find out who she talked to. If she accused anyone. If she said she was close to finding out the secret of what happened to Martha. All of that."

"I don't know. Terry didn't say he had talked to her. I think they've been focused more on searching and seeing if they could find her on the farm."

"I'm sure he's already thought about it, but he's got so much on his mind right now, it could be overlooked. Are we going to go over to the farm after we close today?"

"I don't know. Terry is supposed to update me on what they find. Right now we would probably just be in the way."

Vic's nostrils flared. "This isn't just a job for the men. We can help too."

"I don't think anyone meant that. It's what they do professionally. Our job is the bakery. Their jobs are law enforcement and search and rescue. We'll find out after work what we can do to help them out."

Chapter Eighteen

WHEN ERIN AND VIC did get to the farm, things were eerily quiet. Erin had expected to find the place crawling with people, law enforcement professionals from other agencies and volunteers from town in addition to the little police department, Willie, and Cindy and the friends who had shown up to support her. But there was no one there to stop them and tell them where they could park the car, no volunteer search team being given instructions on how to do a grid search, no crowds of people milling around looking for something to do and waiting for word.

Erin parked the Challenger and walked with Vic to the farmhouse. She waited, watching for the dog, but then saw that he was tied up to the doghouse. As they got out, she saw the fleeting form of the silver-gray cat headed toward the barn. They knocked on the door but then let themselves in.

"Anyone home?" Vic asked.

Cindy was sitting in the living room, along with Lottie Sturm and a couple of other women from town that Erin recognized, but didn't really know. Erin felt awkward about showing up without something in hand. No casserole, no fresh bread or treats from the bakery; she hadn't even thought about what she should do to support Cindy.

Cindy looked at them but didn't demand to know what they were doing there. She didn't chase them back out again, either, which was what Erin had been worried about.

"Uh, hi. We're just wondering... how things are going, and where we can help."

There was no immediate answer. Erin and Vic went into the living room and found places to sit. Erin thought she should give Cindy a comforting squeeze, but she was too far away to do anything.

"Have they... found any sign of Bella?" Erin asked tentatively.

Cindy looked at her for a long time, as if she were far away and had to return to see and hear Erin. "No. They haven't found her. They don't know what happened."

"What do you think happened?" Vic asked. "Do you think she wandered off or got hurt somehow? Do you think someone would take her?"

"Why would anyone take her?"

Vic looked at Erin, silently inquiring about whether she was going to explain.

Erin swallowed. "Because... it could be related to your mother disappearing."

"That's ridiculous, and I told the policeman so," Cindy said strongly. "How could this have anything to do with my mother? She was gone years before Bella was even born."

"If the person who hurt your mother thought that Bella was getting too close to discovering the truth, then they might have... done something."

"This isn't anything to do with my mother."

"So you think she just... had an accident?"

"My mother?"

"Bella. You think that after she put the goats to pasture, she brought the car back to the house, and then disappeared between the parking pad and the house?"

Cindy stared at Vic, unflinching. "You don't know anything about it."

"No. I'm asking."

COUP DE GLACE

"She shouldn't have ever had anything to do with you people. You were putting ideas into her head. Filling her up with your perversions."

"Whoa!" Erin held her hands up to stop Cindy. "Neither of us ever said anything to her about anything but bakery business."

Cindy looked at Erin and Vic, her lip curled in a stubborn sneer.

"Are you saying that Bella was getting ideas from somewhere?" Vic suggested. "Ideas you thought she was getting from work?"

There was another delay in answering. Cindy turned and looked at Lottie Sturm, clearly indicating where the bizarre suggestion about Vic and Erin warping Bella's mind had come from. Erin already knew that Lottie Sturm disapproved of Vic and thought they shouldn't have anything to do with a young girl like Bella.

"She never said anything to me," Cindy admitted.

"Then what?" Vic persisted. "She came home smelling like perfume? Partied late? Brought questionable items into the house?"

"No," Cindy shook her head more definitely. "Nothing like that."

"So you just don't like the fact that she was working with a transgender person. Somebody told you they thought it was a bad idea," Vic looked over at Lottie, raising one eyebrow in question.

"Yes," Cindy agreed. "I just thought it wasn't a good idea."

"You don't think it has anything to do with her disappearing," Erin repeated.

"No."

"What do you think happened, then? Do you think she got confused or hurt? That someone picked her up? What?"

"I don't know." Cindy shook her head. "It's just so unbelievable. She's never done anything like this. She never ran away. She never threatened to run away. She wasn't ever one of those girls who argued and said she hated her mother or that she couldn't stand it anymore and was going to leave. She was never that kind of girl. We always got along together."

"Except she wanted to know what happened to her grandma and grandpa, and you didn't tell her the whole truth."

Cindy looked at Erin with a completely blank expression.

"You didn't fight over it. But she wanted to know things about her grandma and grandpa and you didn't want to talk to her about it."

"I don't know anything about it," Cindy insisted.

"How would your father have reacted if the same thing happened to him? Martha was supposed to be in the garden or the barn, and when he went out to see her, she was gone. And she never, ever came back again." Erin paused. "How do you think that would have made him feel?"

Cindy's gaze sharpened. This wasn't something she'd considered before. Erin was not blaming Ezekiel for Martha's disappearance, but empathizing with how he might have felt if his mate had simply disappeared from the yard one day, never to return again.

"He never said that was what happened," Cindy said.

"Maybe not. But how do you think he would have felt if that was what had happened? How would he have reacted to such a shocking, illogical thing? Would he have called the police about it?"

"Or would he have filled in the blanks," Cindy finished softly. "Would he have just explained it away by saying she had gone to visit someone or to run an errand, and she'd be back soon?"

"It could have happened that way," Erin said. "This might be exactly the same thing that happened to your mother."

COUP DE GLACE

Cindy shook her head. "People don't just disappear into thin air."

"No, they don't," Vic agreed. "So let's start making lists of how she could have disappeared. If this farm swallowed up two people, where did they go?"

Cindy turned her head to look out the window, across the lawn of weeds and drying, hardy grasses, toward the driveway.

"All she had to do is walk across the yard. She couldn't have just fallen into a hole."

"A hole," Vic repeated. "Is there... an old well on the property? A bore hole? A sink hole? A crevasse?"

"There have been several wells," Cindy said, her brow knitting. "One will stop producing, so another is dug..."

"Where are the old wells?" Vic asked. "Are they covered? Filled in?"

"Yes. Of course. It would be too dangerous to leave them open."

"What if the dirt that filled them in has settled or washed away again? What if the hole opened back up?"

"That couldn't happen," Cindy scoffed. "We would have known. We would have seen it."

"But what if you didn't see it. What if someone stepped into it without seeing?"

Cindy shook her head. "They would be hollering for help when we went out looking for them. If a well needed to be filled in twenty years ago... someone would have noticed it."

"You get around here on the roads, mostly. What if it wasn't near a road?"

Cindy continued to shake her head, but Erin thought that Vic had a good point. She pulled out a notebook and wrote down the idea. *Well hole.*

"What about other kinds of holes?" Vic asked. "Anyone digging for oil or mineral deposits? Even just a couple of core samples?" Vic held up her hands, forming a six-inch circle for reference. "Over the years, the rain and erosion could widen it into something much bigger."

"Not on our land."

Erin heard the emphasis on *our*. Maybe Vic was onto something.

"Someone else's land? The Wares or some other neighbor?"

"Robert Ware... his daddy was sure there was riches in the land. Not in growing on it or raising animals on it. But in mineral deposits... underground mines."

"Are there any mines near here?" Vic asked excitedly. "Near the house?"

"No, no. Robert Ware. His daddy wanted to drill holes. What did he call them? Sample holes?"

"Test holes."

Cindy nodded. "Yes. Test holes. On his property."

"Did they find anything?"

Cindy wrinkled her nose. "The Wares are as poor as dirt. Do you think they'd still be living like that if they had found minerals? There's nothing out here but limestone and shale."

"Were there any natural caves?" Erin tried. "Where people go exploring or mining?"

"Spelunking," Vic corrected.

"There's all kinds of caves and tunnels through the mountain," Cindy said. "It's like Swiss cheese. But we fill in any entrances that appear."

At Erin's baffled look, she explained further.

"We fill them in to keep the goats out. Goats are very curious creatures. You don't want a goat falling down into some cave and getting killed or climbing down and getting stuck. Especially not if he calls all of the other goats and they go to see what's happened to him too. When you make a living off of your livestock, you can't take chances. If there are caves or wells or bore holes, we fill them in." Vic and

COUP DE GLACE

Erin followed Cindy's gaze back out the window. "There are no holes between the driveway and the house."

"But what if something attracted Bella's attention," Vic suggested. "What if she saw a cat, or a wounded animal, or some predator, and she chased after it into the woods?" Vic gestured to the thick trees on the other side of the parking pad. "If she ran into the woods and didn't look down in time to see a hole that had opened up…"

"The men have been searching the perimeter of the house all day. What do you think they've been doing?"

A fair question, Erin supposed. She wrote these other options down in her notebook. What if two decades before, the ground had opened up and swallowed Martha Prost? Traumatized, her husband had made up a story to explain her disappearance. No one had ever looked for the hole she had fallen down. Then twenty years later, Bella had walked into the same hole, chasing after the silver-gray cat or something else. It had a certain sense to it.

"A hole like that doesn't need to be very big," Erin said. "You read about young children falling down wells, and they're not talking about big holes two feet across. They're talking about four or six-inch pipes. For an adult Bella's size, that might translate to…?" She looked at Vic for help.

"I have no idea," Vic said apologetically. "But it wouldn't have to look that big. With grass and weeds growing over it, you might not see anything more than a depression in the ground, and not realize that there was a hole."

"We need to do a grid search like on TV," Erin determined, "where they poke sticks into the ground. Like when they're looking for an avalanche victim."

"You think my mother fell into a hole and no one ever found her?" Cindy demanded.

"It's possible. No one combed the woods when she went missing. And in the twenty years since, have you ever done a thorough search of the whole property? There are other options too. A hole is just one possibility. She might have chased after an animal and had a heart attack, and nobody found her body in the thick undergrowth. Scavengers might have—" Vic cut herself off. There was no benefit to filling Cindy's mind with gruesome images. There were large predators in the woods. There were smaller scavengers. Animals that would make short work of a body if allowed to work undisturbed. In a few days, there would be little left but bones, which would quickly be overgrown with foliage.

"Bella didn't have a heart attack," Cindy said. "Bella is as healthy as a horse. She's only seventeen, and she's strong and capable. She wouldn't have gone off chasing something in the woods when it was almost time to go into work. She's always very concerned about getting to the bakery in time."

Erin nodded and gave Cindy a warm smile. "She's a very responsible girl. Very hard worker. You should be proud of that."

Cindy didn't respond with a smile of her own. Erin shouldn't have expected her to. The woman had just lost her daughter. Expecting her to act like a proud, doting parent in the midst of her loss was ridiculous.

"Does anyone trap in these woods?" Vic asked. "Have there been any animal sightings that anyone has been concerned about? She could have gotten caught in a trap someone had put out for a bear or cougar."

"No." Cindy shook her head as if this were just too much. "No one would put traps on our property."

"And Bella wouldn't have gone onto someone else's property?"

Cindy shrugged. "We're not like that with our neighbors. When I was little, Robert Ware would yell at me and threaten me if he thought I'd been on his land. Believe me, I was always careful not to trespass. But he's mellowed out and he's kind to Bella, and nowadays there isn't anyone around here who would give us a lick of trouble for going on a stroll and crossing a property line."

"They're all pretty clearly marked anyway, aren't they?" Erin said, remembering the white fence out past the cemetery. "There are fences."

"My father was always very particular about fences," Cindy agreed, nodding. "He always made sure that they were in good repair, every year, making sure that nothing was broken or cut. If he thought a fence had been moved, even a couple of inches, he would be on the phone and making threats." Cindy gave a little shudder. Not being melodramatic, Erin didn't think. The memory actually did make her cringe.

"Ezekiel had a temper, didn't he?" she asked.

"I thought you believed he didn't know what happened to my mother."

"I do believe it. Or I'm willing to consider it, since there's no real way to know one way or the other. I was just... observing." Erin hesitated to share anything more personal, especially in front of the other women, but decided to chance it. "I was a foster kid," she said. "I've been in more than one home where... the dad was real mean. Sometimes physically abusive, sometimes not. But even the ones who didn't hit still scared the heck out of me."

"We breed them tougher than that out here," Lottie sneered. "It's not like the city where everyone is so sensitive. You can't raise your voice at a child these days without being accused of being abusive."

Erin had been watching Cindy for her reaction. Cindy looked toward her friend, but didn't agree with her comments. Her face remained a mask. She looked at Erin.

"He had a temper," she agreed, ignoring the rest of the conversation. "That doesn't mean he would have done anything to my mother, I could never picture him killing in a fit of rage. He'd never struck her in front of me. But he was very... opinionated, and very protective of the family's property and rights. He wasn't about to let anything interfere with the running of the farm and our ability to make a living. He and the neighbors were often getting into fights over boundary lines, water rights, timber, deadfall... In the time that it's been just me and Bella here, it's been much quieter. We have a much better relationship with the neighbors now, more cooperative instead of competitive." She shrugged. "With men, it's all about who's the bigger dog. Women do things differently. Daddy might not have approved of how I've handled negotiations, but I think he'd be happy with the farm and the way that it's running."

Erin tried to picture Ezekiel and how he had related to his family, neighbors, and the townspeople. The tall, spare man she had seen in the pictures had not been a self-effacing, soft-spoken farmer. He'd been an alpha male, standing guard over his territory, making sure his family and property were protected. How would he have reacted if Martha had said she was leaving him? The children were gone, and it was just the two of them; maybe she had decided the situation had become intractable. She had no more reason to stay with him.

But that didn't fit the facts. Not if Bella's disappearance was related to the disappearance of her grandmother. It was an accident or mishap. A fall, an unexpected injury. Or maybe something darker—was it possible there had been something more malevolent at work? Blackmail, jealousy, an affair. Some secret that was still important to keep even twenty years later. She'd seen it play out several times in Bald Eagle Falls. What made them think that Martha Prost's disappearance was any different?

"When you went through your parents' things after your dad died, was there any hint that either of them had had an affair? Or had been hiding some other secret?"

Cindy rolled her eyes. "Now the smear campaign starts. I thought you were going to be different because you said he might not have done it, but you're just going right back to it all being his fault."

"No, I'm not," Erin protested. "I'm just looking at the facts, trying to figure out what might have happened."

"Bella's disappearance has nothing to do with my father. He died almost twenty years ago. I don't know why Bell was so obsessed with the two of them lately. It's a dark part of my life I would like to just forget. I don't understand why she needed to bring it all up and make a big deal of it. Some things are better just forgotten"

Chapter Nineteen

It was a long day, especially since Vic and Erin had started so early and had been working extra hours lately getting the freezer stocked. They met with Terry and Willie and the others who were in the police department or had been asked to help with the search, coming in from the forests surrounding the farm house as night fell and they couldn't continue their search. Their faces were grim, voices low. They obviously had not found Bella nor any clear sign of what had happened to her. K9 nosed at Erin and whined when he saw her, not something he usually did. He was obviously just as tired and footsore as the men. Erin rubbed his head and fetched a water bottle out of the car for him to drink. Terry looked down at K9 as Erin fussed over him, obviously too exhausted to do anything.

"You didn't find anything?" Erin asked, even though it was clear in their faces. "No sign of what happened?"

Terry slid the backpack he wore off his shoulder and dug out a bag. "Was this Bella's?"

Erin looked down at the locket in the evidence bag. "That was her grandma's."

Terry's shoulders sagged. "Her grandma's? It hasn't been out in the elements for twenty years. It's not weathered."

"No. It was in Cindy's bedroom before. Bella got it out for Reg, when she wanted something to... help her connect with Grandma Prost's ghost." Erin gave an uncomfortable shrug, an attempt to apologize for Reg's actions.

COUP DE GLACE

"When was this?"

"The day that Reg and I came out here. Last Friday."

"Did she drop it that day? Lose it somewhere?"

"No, not that she mentioned. I remember her taking it back from Reg in the barn, but after that… she must have put it in her pocket."

"Did you see her with it any time after that? Did she wear it?"

Erin closed her eyes, trying to envision it. Ask her about smells and tastes, and she could recollect perfectly. Visual input was harder for her. Bella hadn't talked about the locket again after that, Erin was pretty sure of that. But had she worn it?

"I don't know," she said. "We don't wear jewelry while we're baking. Anything we wear has to be taken off, so Vic and I don't generally bother to wear anything in. Bella comes here after school, so sometimes she has jewelry that needs to be removed. She's pretty good about remembering to do it before she starts to work." Erin tried to picture Bella taking the locket off and putting it into the pencil box she used to corral such odds and ends. She could see rings and bracelets in her mind's eye, but not the locket. "No… I don't remember her wearing it."

"How about when you were out here with Vic. You guys toured all the main points of interest?"

"Yes. We started at the house, and then she gave us a tour around the property. The pastures, the goat barn, all that. Where did you find the locket?"

"Was she wearing it that day?"

"I don't think so. She didn't want her mom to know that she had taken it the day that Reg was here, so I would have expected her just to put it back in the jewelry box. I don't remember ever seeing her wearing it."

"But she could have had it under her shirt instead of over."

"Yes, sure. No one would know it was anything other than a chain."

"Or Cindy could have been wearing it," Vic suggested. "It was hers."

Terry nodded slowly. "It's a possibility," he agreed. "How much did she tell you about her mother's disappearance?"

"The basics," Erin told him. "I didn't feel like she was telling us everything. Maybe that's not fair, but I thought there was more to it than she would say… especially about her dad. Not necessarily that he knew what had happened to her mother or had been involved, just that… there was a lot of family history that she didn't want to talk about. Things about her dad. Maybe about both of them."

"History of domestic violence?"

"She said he had never hit Martha in front of Cindy. But she's ambivalent on whether she thought he was violent with her in private. He was a disciplinarian when Cindy was a child. Physically punished her."

"Are you going to organize a bigger search in the morning?" Vic asked. "Get volunteers from town and do a grid search? I wondered if she could have had an accident, fallen down an old well or a crevasse…"

"Maybe." Terry wiped his forehead with the back of his hand, looking utterly exhausted. "We'll have to decide that in the next few hours."

"Where did you find the necklace?" Erin asked. "Was it near the house?"

"No."

"I'm amazed you found it. With all of the thick underbrush, it could have disappeared forever. Cindy will be very glad you found it."

Terry said nothing.

"It was…" Erin tried to pin down further details. "Was it dropped along a pathway? Or did it get caught on something? Is it broken?" Erin hadn't even thought to look when Terry had shown it to her.

"It isn't broken," Terry advised. "It wasn't caught or torn off."

Erin felt her body loosen a little, relieved that there was no indication of violence.

"So it just fell out of her pocket while she was working. Do you think she lost it today? Or sometime in the last few days?"

Terry hesitated, seriously considering his answer. Erin looked over at Vic to see if she thought this was odd behavior.

"It wasn't dropped," Terry said finally. "It appeared to be deliberately placed."

"Deliberately…?"

"It was looped around the corner of Ezekiel's gravestone."

Erin blinked, surprised by this. Eventually, she shrugged. "I guess that's a logical place to put it. Sort of a memorial for Martha, reuniting her and Ezekiel. Reg told Bella they should be together, but no one knows what happened to Martha, so she couldn't be interred there…"

Something tickled at the back of Erin's brain, but she couldn't quite grasp it. She shook her head.

"She didn't do that the day we were up there," Vic said.

"No, not that I saw," Erin agreed. "She must have gone back and done it after that."

"Today?" Terry asked.

"She wouldn't have had time today. Not if she had to take the goats out to pasture and then come in to the bakery. There wouldn't have been time to go all the way up to the cemetery."

"She was already there. It wouldn't have taken more than a minute."

Erin frowned. "Why was she there?"

"To take the goats to pasture."

"To… the upper pasture?"

"Yes. That's where she took the goats this morning."

"I thought she took them to the lower pasture. That's where they were the day when we were here."

"The grass was long in the upper pasture," Vic said. "They hadn't been up there for quite a while. They must have been finished in the lower pasture, so Bella took them up instead."

Erin nodded. "Right. No reason why they wouldn't. I was just picturing that she'd gone to the lower pasture."

Vic looked at Erin, and Erin looked at her. Terry sensed the tension and waited for Erin and Vic to work it out and tell him what was going on. Erin couldn't shake the vague sense of unease she felt, knowing that Bella had gone to the upper pasture instead of the lower.

"What is it?"

"Nothing. When we were up there, we saw one of their neighbors, Mr. Ware. The fence between their two properties is up there."

Terry nodded. "We'll talk to neighbors. Today we just checked whether anyone had seen Bella. We'll have to interview them more deeply later."

"He seemed nice," Vic said.

"Yes. And Cindy said she hasn't had any trouble with them since Ezekiel died," Erin contributed.

Terry scratched his chin. "But Ezekiel and he had issues?"

"Just some competitiveness. Territoriality…"

"Had there been any dispute over property rights lately?"

"Cindy said not. She said everything has been quiet, there haven't been any issues."

Terry nodded. "I'll talk to Cindy about the necklace, maybe she knows whether Bella was wearing it today or whether she left it in the cemetery sometime last week. We can't assume it means anything at all if she wasn't wearing it today."

Erin had crawled into bed much later than her usual bedtime. Vic planned to take a sleeping pill so that she'd be able to get in a few hours before morning. Terry wasn't headed to bed, but he didn't need to be up as early as they did, either. The townspeople would not be ready to start a search until a decent hour. They all separated, going their different directions. Erin lay in bed, patting Orange Blossom and making notes in her notepad as she waited for her brain to start winding down so that she'd be able to sleep.

She didn't like to take sleeping pills, which always left her feeling groggy and hung over in the morning. She had an herbal tea Adele had left with her earlier, along with some valerian, hoping she'd be able to settle in for sleep, which seemed a long way off.

Orange Blossom purred and snored. Erin tried to match her breaths to his, resting her eyes.

She started to doze with the bedside lamp still on, unwilling to turn it off until she knew for sure she'd be able to fall asleep. She didn't want to toss and turn in the darkness, getting increasingly frustrated.

Her restless, waking dreams took her back to the meeting in the barn. She saw all of them as if from up above. Reg, Bella, and herself. Reg twirled and hummed and called for Grandma Prost to come, holding the locket up over her head like a beacon or a lightning rod. She heard the rustling of wings and the low murmur of the birds as they called to each other and watched the bizarre show going on down below.

"Grandma Prost," Reg chanted, "come and commune with us. Bella wants to talk to you."

"Leave me alone," Erin said from her viewpoint up above them. "Why don't you leave me in peace?"

"You can't stay in the barn," Bella told her. "Mom said. It's not allowed. It's too dangerous in here."

Erin tried to explain that she didn't know where she was, and Reg shook her head, sending her skinny braids dancing around her head. "Ghosts belong in the graveyard. Not the house. Not the barn. The graveyard."

Erin felt herself being pulled away from the barn. She tried to hold on, but there was nothing for her to grasp. The tug that started behind her belly button increased until she felt sick, and she had to let herself be pulled by it. She stared up at the stars and tried to count them. She looked for the familiar constellations but couldn't find them.

"You're on the other side," Reg told her, "so they're backwards."

Erin tried looking for their mirror images, but still couldn't find them.

"Count goats," Bella told her, "they're much healthier than sheep."

Erin tried to gather the stars to her but couldn't gather them together. Looking more closely, she saw that they were goats, and they followed behind Bella, bleating and complaining about the way they had been treated.

"You didn't put the goats away," she told Bella.

"I couldn't. He took me away before I could."

"Who did?"

"Pan. The goatherd."

Erin blinked. Her eyes were sticky, and she couldn't quite wake up.

"Where did Pan take the goats?"

"Over here." Bella led her to the cemetery, which was much larger than it had seemed when Erin had been there in real life. It went on forever, with rows and rows of crosses and tombstones, and many statues of sheep and goats and angels. A lot of the angels seemed to have pig snouts.

"I told you not to bring the pigs," Erin told them. There was no answer. She started to wander up and down the aisles, looking for the others. "Where did you guys go? Are you going to leave me here forever?"

"It is forever," Reg told her gently. "A ghost can't come back. You can talk to us, but you have to stay there forever."

Erin shivered as a cold wind blew through her. "But it's cold here. I don't want to stay here. Can't I go in the house, where it's warmer?" She remembered the barn that she had come from. "I'll go back to the barn. I'll stay there, and I promise I won't bother anyone."

"The grave is always cold," Bella said. "Wherever it is. You take the cold with you."

Erin didn't think that was true. She tried to push her way out of the cold, to look outside of the graveyard and see back through the stars to the barn again.

"It's getting smaller," Bella said. "We're getting bigger, so it's getting smaller."

And it was. She could see the white boundary fences around the cemetery. She could count the rows and columns that before had seemed endless. Erin tried to touch one of the grave markers. She could see Bella's name on it. On the one beside that, she could see Clementine's name, and then her parents. Erin hadn't realized that her family was buried in that cemetery. She'd never seen the gravestones before.

The tombstones were just beyond her reach. Every time she tried to touch them, the distance changed, and then she was standing at the edge of the cemetery where there were no new markers. While she watched, a hole opened up in the ground. First it was round, like an animal burrow, but it got bigger and bigger until she was afraid she could fall into it. As it expanded, it took on a rectangular shape, until she knew she was looking at a grave.

"You'll be fine here," Bella said tenderly. "Goodbye, Erin."

"I don't want this one," Erin objected, looking around. "I want to be buried with my family."

"They're here. Don't you worry. This is the right place."

"No. I don't want this. I still have to make the mud pies."

"The mud pies will always be there. They'll make themselves. This is your place."

As Erin watched, the rectangular hole started to fill in, and she knew it was her grave and she was already in it. They were going to bury her, whether she was ready or not.

"Wait," she insisted. "This isn't right. Wait until I'm ready."

"Death waits for no man," a man's voice insisted. "This is where you will be, until the angel blows the trump."

Erin looked at the gravestones around her, at all of the cherubs with pig noses waiting to blow the trump.

"I don't want to."

"You belong here."

The grave had filled with dirt. Grass grew over top of it, but Erin could still see the outline in the grass, the slight depression where the dirt had settled over time.

Chapter Twenty

THE MORNING ALARM WENT off, making Erin's whole body convulse with surprise and panic. What had happened? What had she done? Where was she, and why couldn't she just run away again?

The bedroom at Clementine's house resolved around her. She was home. It had just been one of those restless dreams like she had when she was camping or wasn't able to get to sleep at the right time. How much had she managed to get in? A couple of hours? Not nearly enough, but she needed to get up and get moving anyway. She would catch up on her sleep the coming nights. The searchers would need to be fed. Something sturdy and portable, like the energy bars she made for hikers. People who were upset about Bella's disappearance would want comfort food. And she needed to replace at least some of the many popsicles and frozen treats that had been consumed the day before.

Erin forced herself to swing her feet off the edge of the bed to start her on her way to the bathroom where she would shower to wake herself up. Orange Blossom stretched all of his legs out and opened his mouth in an incredibly wide yawn that ended with a tiny squeak. She smiled and shook her head at him.

"You're just trying to be cute, aren't you?"

He curled himself into a ball and looked at her upside-down. He would go back to sleep while Erin was in the shower, but once she was dressed, he would trip her all the way to the kitchen, yowling and complaining like he hadn't been fed in days.

By the time the animals were fed, and the tea kettle was whistling, Vic had made it into the kitchen. She yawned almost as widely as Orange Blossom and covered her mouth after it was done.

"Some mornings come way too soon," she commented. "Whose idea was it to become a baker, anyway?"

"I feel like I was up all night," Erin said. "The dreams that I was having... you couldn't have made up anything more bizarre."

"I slept like the dead."

Erin had to laugh at the turn of phrase, after the subject of her dreams. "I guess I did too, but not the kind of dead who just go to sleep and stay there!"

Vic gave her a quizzical smile. "But you don't believe in any other kind of dead, do you? You think that once a person dies, that's it and they're gone from this earth for good, don't you?"

"Yes. Other than the legacies they leave behind. I don't believe in an eternal spirit... but I did dream that I was one last night."

"You dreamed something you don't believe in? Doesn't that tell you something?"

"I've dreamed about being able to fly or breathe underwater, but I didn't wake up being able to do those things!"

Vic considered. "Well, yeah, I suppose."

Erin took a sip of her tea that had not yet had enough time to steep. She made a face and put it to the side. "I think I was Bella's grandmother, at least for part of the dreams. I could see myself from outside, because I was a ghost."

"Uh-huh."

Erin did her best to remember and describe the progression of the dream to Vic. It was already slipping away from her, in the way that dreams did, and in a few days, she probably wouldn't be able to remember any of it. She described the filling and settling of the earth inside the grave.

Vic nodded. "That's pretty macabre. I guess your brain was disturbed from everything that we talked about yesterday. Worry about Bella."

Erin frowned. She took another sip of her tea, trying to get her fuzzy brain to complete her mental processes.

"Whose grave was next to Ezekiel's?"

"I don't know... I guess his parents on one side. And then a plot beside him for Martha. But like Bella said, they didn't have any remains to bury there, so it was still empty."

"Then why would they dig it up?"

Vic shook her head. "They didn't. They didn't even put up a memorial headstone. If it was me, I would have at least put up a headstone, even if no one ever found my wife. It's just the right thing to do."

"The empty plot was to the right."

"Uh-huh."

"The ground had settled. There was a rectangle of ground that was lower by an inch."

Vic opened her mouth to answer, and then she understood. "Like it had been dug out and refilled, and then the ground had settled. But there would be no need to do that if there was no body to bury."

Erin nodded.

"You don't think someone...?"

Erin nodded again.

"We'd better call Terry!"

"Let him sleep. He won't be able to get anything done this early in the morning. He'll have to wait until everyone else is up anyway."

Terry came by the bakery later in the morning to let Erin know what was going on and what their plans were for the day. As Erin had anticipated, portable snacks and meals would be wanted, and she already had rows of granola and energy bars molded and ready to be wrapped. She tentatively explained to Terry about the empty plot next to Ezekiel's, which she suspected wasn't quite as empty as they had thought. He frowned, thinking back to his investigation of the day before.

"I was so focused on the necklace on Ezekiel's headstone, I never even looked at the empty plot," he said. "It never even registered."

"I didn't really think about it either, but I guess I noticed it subconsciously. Who would have done it, though?" Erin asked. "Cindy? I don't think Bella knew. I don't think it could have been Ezekiel, because if it was him, wouldn't he have put his wife in the next plot in line, not leaving a space for himself and then burying her in the next one?"

"First of all, you're jumping to conclusions by assuming it is Martha in that grave, if it even is a grave. And if it is, it could be an old one, from generations ago."

"Why would somebody have skipped over the plots for Ezekiel and his parents and whoever else generations ago? They wouldn't just put people in random places in the graveyard. They would have followed some kind of order or pattern."

"There may be a logical layout we don't know about. More questions than can be answered right now. I'll talk to Cindy and see what she knows. She may be able to explain it. We don't want to waste time on something that might be totally unrelated to the disappearances of Bella and her grandmother."

"Yeah. You're right, I guess. What did you find out from Cindy about the locket?"

"She wasn't even aware that Bella had it. She doesn't know when Bella might have put it on the gravestone."

"So maybe yesterday, maybe not."

Terry nodded. "And does it make any difference? What if she did put it on the grave yesterday? We already know that she was up there, she's the one who took the goats to graze. The necklace doesn't prove anything."

"What if Bella was seen putting it on the grave? What if someone took her because of that?"

"Why?"

"Because... they thought it meant she knew about Martha being buried there. Or maybe she said something to someone about the grave next to it."

"Maybe," Terry said, giving a hesitant shrug.

"When we were up there with her, she said it didn't look right."

"What didn't look right?"

"She didn't know. She said maybe it was because she hadn't been there for a while. But maybe she figured it out yesterday, like I did in my dream."

"Who was there when she said it didn't look right?"

"Just me and Vic. Mr. Ware was there for a little while too. I don't remember what parts of the conversation he was there for."

The first order of business was to take Cindy to the cemetery to see if she noticed anything out of place. She kept asking what was wrong and what she was supposed to see, but Terry shook his head and asked her to just look around. He looked at the depression in the ground in the plot next to Ezekiel's and looked at Erin. She hadn't imagined it. That part hadn't just been a dream. It had been a memory that her brain had been working away at, trying to tell her that something was wrong.

But Cindy barely even glanced in the direction of the plot. She looked at her father's headstone. She looked around at a few others, which apparently all looked just the same as they always had. She looked around, staring off into the distance, where Erin could see the white fence between the Prost farm and the Ware property.

"It seems so much smaller," she said, gazing around the cemetery again.

"That's what Bella said," Erin agreed. "She said it must be because she hadn't been there for a long time. Like when you go back somewhere you knew when you were a little kid, and it's so much smaller than it was, because you're bigger." Erin had felt much the same way when she had seen Clementine's shop again. *It was only that big? Hadn't it once been much bigger and grander?*

"Yes," Cindy agreed. "That must be it."

They all stood there quietly.

"That fence is new," Cindy said finally.

"Mr. Ware must have replaced it in just the last few years."

"Maybe. I don't think I've been up here since Ezekiel was buried."

"Seventeen years ago?"

"More or less."

"Cindy…" Erin ventured.

"What?"

"You said that Ezekiel used to fight over the property lines. When he thought fences had been moved, even just a few inches."

"Yes."

"Was it Mr. Ware he got angry with?"

"Any of the neighbors… but yes, he and Mr. Ware had a number of arguments over boundaries and land rights."

"And that new fence… is it in the same place as the old fence?"

Cindy studied it, considering, before slowly shaking her head.

Chapter Twenty-One

"NO, THAT'S NOT WHERE the old fence was," Cindy said slowly. "It's much closer."

"And you don't know when he put it up?"

"No. He keeps the grounds," she motioned to the cemetery, "so that I don't have to. I always thought it was very kind of him. Not like he was when I was a little girl and he was always angry and yelling at us."

Eliminating the need for Cindy to go to the cemetery herself. She obviously didn't visit her father's grave.

"But why would he move the fence line?" Cindy asked. "Who cares where the fence is?"

"Your father did."

"I know, but he was fussy about things like that. I never could understand why it mattered. So what if it's not exactly on the property line? That doesn't change anything. Just because he moves the fence, that doesn't mean he moves the boundary."

Erin frowned and looked at Terry. He pursed his lips. "Actually, Miss Prost, it can."

"Whatever do you mean?"

"It's something called adverse possession. Squatter's rights."

"He wasn't living on our land. He can't claim that."

"No. But if you don't object to the placement of his fence line, and it remains there for twenty years, he can claim adverse possession and get the legal property line moved."

Cindy stared at him blankly at first, then as she gradually processed what Terry had said, her face turned into a mask of fury. She cussed Mr. Ware out. "He's trying to steal my property? That's the reason he's been so nice and offered to do the cemetery for me? So he could steal my property?" She shook her head. "Why would he? What makes an acre of my property so valuable to him? It's not even cleared to pasture."

Terry gazed toward the fence line. "Why don't we take a look?"

They all moved toward the new fence. Erin thought about how Mr. Ware had previously approached them when they were at the cemetery, demanding to know who was there as if it were his own land. Had he been worried that Bella had noticed something out of place? That one of them would wonder about the grave next to Ezekiel's? Or had Bella gone back there after taking the goats to the upper pasture, placing the necklace on her grandfather's tombstone and he had struck her down while she knelt over the grave?

She was nervous and wanted to take Terry's hand for comfort, but he didn't even seem to be aware of her as he marched through the trees, eyes ahead on the fence line. Cindy was still muttering angrily, bristling like an angry dog. They both moved faster than Erin, more used to tramping through the wilds, more confident of themselves than Erin. They climbed over the fence. K9 slipped under it. They moved in opposite directions, looking for something to indicate why Mr. Ware would want to add that land to his property. Surely it couldn't be just more forest.

Erin stopped at the fence, loath to go over and trespass on Mr. Ware's land. But it wasn't Mr. Ware's land, it was Cindy's. She had gone over the fence without a second thought. "Do you see anything?"

Terry glanced in her direction briefly but didn't answer. He watched K9 sniff around and studied the ground. Erin climbed over the fence, still feeling like she was invading Mr. Ware's space, though she logically knew that she wasn't, and he wasn't going to come and run her off his land like a child who'd stepped on the neighbor's lawn.

Terry was looking down and appeared to be following something along the ground. Erin followed a distance behind. She wondered where the actual boundary line was and looked for the old fence posts or holes where they had been. But if it had been ten years or more since the new fence was erected, any sign of the old fence would be long gone.

K9 barked and Terry hurried after him. It wasn't an alarming sound; Erin didn't think it meant that he had found anything worrisome, but something had caught his interest. Cindy had ranged off to the right, and when she heard K9 bark and saw Terry follow him, she hurried after him.

"What is it? What did you find?"

They disappeared behind a hillock and a stand of trees and brambles. Erin picked up her pace, not wanting to be left behind. She got close enough to see Terry kneeling down and Cindy leaning over.

"Some kind of cave," Terry was saying.

There was the snap of a twig behind Erin, making her jump.

Erin turned her head quickly.

It was Mr. Ware. Not the smiling, chuckling tease this time. His face was red, and he held a big heavy handgun that looked like it might have been used during the civil war. It was pointed at Erin.

"You're trespassing on private property," he growled.

Erin swallowed and cleared her throat, having difficulty getting the words out. "It's Prost property. Cindy's right there..." Erin gestured, before thinking better of it and thinking that maybe she shouldn't have pointed to where Cindy and Terry were crouched. But it was too late to take it back, Mr. Ware was already looking at the additional intruders, his brows squeezing down in a heavy scowl.

"Get your hands up, all of you," Mr. Ware shouted, loudly enough that Cindy and Terry heard and looked up to see what was going on.

Erin raised her hands tentatively. She didn't know if that was the correct response, but she wasn't armed and didn't want him to think she was. Her heart was pounding so hard she was sure everyone must be able to hear it.

She had turned to look back at Cindy and Terry to see what they were going to do and make sure that they had heard Mr. Ware. In a couple of seconds, Mr. Ware had closed the distance between them and wrapped one long arm around her, pulling her against him.

"Don't do anything stupid," Terry warned in a calm, reasonable voice. "Stop and think things through. You don't want to be in more trouble than you are already in. Threatening people isn't going to help anything. Let's just all back off and take a breath while we think this over."

"You back off. Right off of my property."

"Your property?" Cindy screeched. "This is my property! Just because you put a fence on it, that doesn't make it your property. My daddy was always on the lookout for people like you, trying to take what wasn't theirs. I should have remembered that. I should have been watching out for you too!"

"Your daddy was a pain in the neck," Mr. Ware said. "He was paranoid about those stupid fences. What did he think he was protecting? More pasture land for the goats? There isn't anything out here that's worth fighting over."

Was there really not anything of value on the other side of the fence? Had he just misjudged the property line?

Terry made a calming motion with his hands. "Let's just talk about this. Let go of Erin, and we can all have a civilized conversation. If there's any confusion over where the boundary line is, we can get a surveyor out here to establish it. There's no need to go to such lengths…"

"Nothing out here worth fighting for?" Cindy spat. "What's this, then?" She gestured at the ground. "If there isn't anything on my property that you want, then why did you move the fence?"

"What? There isn't anything over there. You people think every fox hole is a buried treasure. It's worthless land. Just more trees and weeds."

Mr. Ware was clearly bluffing.

Terry was watching Erin and Mr. Ware, assessing the situation, but he couldn't help dropping his eyes to the ground too, studying whatever he and Cindy could see there.

"I think there might be more to this," he said. "It's more a cave than a fox hole, and there's a path worn in the ground. That means someone has been traveling over this path repeatedly. There's only one thing I can think of that makes someone keep going back to a hole in the ground."

"I don't know who you think you are, cop, but you can go back to the city and forget you were ever here. This is my property."

"It's my property!" Cindy argued back. "And this mine—if that's what it is—is on my property. And I want to know what happened to my daughter! What did you do to her?"

"You mean did she come snooping around here just like her mother?" Mr. Ware tightened his grip on Erin, his arm so tight around her that it hurt. She breathed shallowly. "You all think you can just come around here and poke your noses into my business? My legitimate and rightful business?"

Terry started moving toward Erin and Mr. Ware. Erin stayed as still as possible, worried about the big gun.

"You can just stay back there, young fella," Ware growled.

"I thought you told me to get off of the property. I need to go back the way I came if I'm going to do that."

Ware considered it for a moment. "Cindy first," he said. "Get out of here and stay out. And you, just stay where you are, or I'm going to use this thing." He waggled the gun in his hand to show it off. "Let me tell you, the mess that it leaves behind isn't going to be pretty."

"No need to make any threats," Terry assured him. "I'll stay still. Miss Prost, I want you to do what he says. Go back to your car. We don't want any violence."

"You think there hasn't already been violence here?" Cindy's voice was a howl. "Where is my daughter? What have you done with her?"

"Just get out of here, woman! I never could abide the Prost women and their never-ending nosiness! Why can't you just stay at the farmhouse and mind your own business?"

Did he mean Grandma Prost? Bella? Cindy herself?

Cindy had, Erin was relieved to note, begun to walk back toward the cemetery and her car, though not at all happy about it. Ware pulled Erin off the barely discernible path, causing her to stumble, so that Cindy could walk by. After Cindy walked past him, Ware looked back at Terry.

"Take off your gun and drop it on the ground."

Terry didn't protest, but immediately did what he was told, unsnapping his service weapon, removing it from the holster, and dropping it on the ground. K9 whined and sniffed at the gun, concerned about his master's strange behavior. Terry stood with his hands at his sides, looking calm and relaxed. "You're in charge," he said. "Should I go with Cindy now?"

Ware nodded. "Walk slowly, and if that dog makes even a twitch toward me, I'm going to blow him away."

As worried as Erin was for her own safety, she didn't want anything to happen to K9. The dog was Terry's loyal

COUP DE GLACE

partner and she couldn't bear to see anything happen to him.

Terry looked at Erin, his eyes unreadable dark holes. She knew he would do whatever he could for her, but she didn't know what he could do. Would Ware let her go once the others were off of 'his' property? Erin had a pretty good idea that he wasn't going to be satisfied there. He knew as well as they did that kicking them off the property wasn't going to make it his. It wasn't going to keep anyone from returning.

"Can I go now?" Erin asked, her voice quavering even though she tried to keep it strong.

Ware looked toward the cave, uncertain. "Did they go inside?"

"No. No, they just came over and saw the hole. No one went in."

One strong arm around her and the gun jabbing painfully into her side, Ware dragged her over to the hollow that Terry and Cindy had been in. Erin averted her eyes, not wanting to see the cave. If she didn't see it, he couldn't kill her for being a witness. He could let her go, knowing that she wouldn't be able to tell anyone anything.

"Doesn't look like much of anything, does it?" Ware asked his hot breath in her ear. He bodily turned her toward it. Erin stopped trying to look away and obeyed him, looking down.

It didn't look like a cave or a mine. Erin had been spelunking with Vic and Willie and Terry, and she had been in the entrance of one of Willie's mines. But neither experience would have led her to believe that the crevice in the ground was anything of importance.

"Get down and take a look," Ware told her.

"I... I don't want to."

"Get down." He pushed her away from him, throwing her down with surprising force. He might be an old man, but he wasn't weak and frail. "You're the one who started all of this, asking questions about what was none of your business. So you take a look."

Erin was on her hands and knees. She reached out and swept her hand through the long grasses and wild plants to find the entrance. What had looked like just a small hole and a twisting crack in the soil was actually much bigger, it had simply been camouflaged by all of the overgrown weeds. Erin parted them, crawling forward on her knees, to reveal a hole large enough for a man or woman to crawl in through. She nodded and backed up.

"Yes... I see it now. I'm sorry to have bothered you. I don't want to stay here anymore. I'll leave you alone. You can..." she waved her hands at the cave, "do whatever."

"Go inside. Have a look around."

Erin felt like she was choking just at the thought. "I don't like caves," she confessed. "I don't want to go inside."

He smiled at her words. "Crawl in. It's bigger inside."

"I can't. I was hurt in a cave once. I can't do it."

He put his booted foot on her backside and shoved her. Erin fell on her face. A red and yellow lightning of pain shot from her face into her brain and, for a moment, she could see nothing else. She pushed herself back up, grit in her mouth, afraid that she'd broken her teeth or her nose. She tried not to inhale through her nose, afraid of sucking in blood. She crawled forward, finding her way more by feel than by sight.

"Please," she begged.

He didn't capitulate. Erin crawled farther in, feeling rocks under her knees, blinking and hoping that her eyes would get used to the dimness inside and that she wouldn't be left in total darkness. Not again. Erin tried to breathe slowly, finding herself gasping, already worried that she was running out of air. When she had been lost in the caves before, Willie had brought oxygen. Where was Willie now? Why hadn't they found the cave when they had searched for Bella the previous day?

COUP DE GLACE

Because they had not known to search beyond the marked boundaries of the property. They hadn't realized that the fence was in the wrong place. How were they to know? How would anyone other than the Prosts know?

"That's far enough," Erin said. "Please. It's dark. I can't see. I can't breathe."

He threw something at her that hit her in the elbow and made the nerve tingle all the way up to her fingertips. At first, she was disconcerted, thinking he had thrown the gun at her. Then she realized it was a flashlight. He had no intention of letting her come out, he wanted her to go farther. He wanted her to see what she was being consigned to.

Erin fumbled with the flashlight. She found the switch and used both hands to get it turned on. She shone it around her and was surprised to see that she wasn't in a narrow tunnel, but a large room. A natural cave. Tall enough for a person to stand up in. She looked back at Ware, who was in the narrower cave entrance behind her, holding the gun on her.

"It's... big."

"Yeah, and this is just the front lobby." He crawled in and then got to his feet. He pointed to a tunnel that branched off to the right. "Over there. Take that one."

Erin shuffled forward. She didn't want to trip and fall. Her face was already throbbing. So were her knees and palms. Her elbow was numb. She didn't want to go any farther. What if he only wanted her to go in so that he could kill her and leave her dead body there, perhaps never to be discovered, like Grandma Prost? Had he walked Bella into the same cave the day before? How many women did he think he could kidnap? Surely, he understood that the police were onto him and there was no longer any escape. Cindy and Terry knew what he had done. They had seen him take Erin. Only a lunatic would think he could get away with further violence.

"I'm tired," Erin protested. She touched her face. "I'm hurt. It's bleeding. Can't I go home now?"

"No. Take that passage."

"I don't like caves. I can't breathe in here." Her breaths were coming in short, sharp gasps. With the two of them in there, the air couldn't last for long. "Please just let me go."

He shoved her. Erin didn't fall, but she was afraid that she was going to stumble over her feet and take another face-plant. She shuffled forward, aiming for the passage Ware pointed to. She probed the darkness with the flashlight, trying to see what she was walking into as far ahead of time as she could. What was she going to find down there? Bones? A decayed body? Rats? Bats? She felt suddenly woozy, and before she knew what was happening, Ware had caught her and lowered her to the cave floor, pulling the flashlight away from her.

Erin covered her mouth, trying not to vomit. Her breathing was so fast she could no longer control it at all. She hunched over, her arm over her stomach and her hand over her mouth.

"You really *don't* like caves, do you?" Ware asked, chuckling.

"No."

Chapter Twenty-Two

HE LET HER KNEEL there for a few minutes, then grasped her arm and pulled her to her feet.

"Please let me go home," Erin urged.

"Just shut your whining. Come with me."

Her body moved automatically as he pulled her along, putting out one foot and then the other to keep her from falling, but all the while she just wanted to curl up and cry.

The tunnel was narrower than the big room Ware had called the front lobby. Erin could feel it closing in around her. She still felt dizzy and sick, but Ware ignored her moans and drunken swaying, taking her down the passage.

They kept going. Erin saw tools along the way. She saw areas where there had been chunks taken out of the walls, though whether with a pickaxe or explosives, she didn't know. She could see darker striations running through the rocks, but she didn't know what she was seeing. Willie would have known. He was the miner. He would have been in heaven in the little underground cave system. It was just the type of place he was always looking for.

"What is it?" Erin asked. "What kind of mine?"

"Most of what you find in Tennessee ain't worth spit," Ware told her, and he spat on the rock floor in front of them to emphasize his point. "Semi-precious quartz, copper, bitumen. You can cart it out of here your whole life and not make enough to keep body and soul together. But every now and then, you find something else. You won't find diamonds or sapphires in here, like in South Carolina. But you can find gold."

"Gold?" Erin stared at one of the darker striations. "Is that what that is?"

"Nah. The gold is deeper down. There's a whole little world down here. You could walk through these passages your whole life and not find your way out. This system probably runs under half of Tennessee."

Erin felt the walls closing around her again. She could picture the labyrinthine tunnels he described. She'd seen them before. She could have died down there, and maybe she still would.

"I've seen your cave," Erin moaned. "Please let me go now."

Ware shook his head at her. "Don't you have any spirit of adventure? Even that stupid girl at least took some interest in seeing what was down here."

"Bella?" Erin croaked. "Did you bring her down here? What did you do with her? Where is she?"

"Do you want me to take you to see her?"

Erin held both hands over her stomach. "No! Yes. I don't want to see her if she's dead. Did you kill her?"

"I've never killed a thing intentionally in my life." He paused for her reaction. "Can you believe that? Living out here in the wilderness, and I never once shot a deer. Not even a rabbit or a thieving raccoon. I'll tell you, my pappy wasn't too impressed with me. What's wrong with a boy who doesn't want to go out hunting or fishing? Back then, it was a matter of life and death. There wasn't no grocery store where you could just go pick up whatever you needed. You ate what you got for yourself, and sometimes one deer was all that stood between you and starvation."

"That must have been very hard."

"Pappy whipped the hide offa me, trying to get me to give up my sissy ideas and help provide for the family. But that just convinced me all the more that I didn't want anything to do with causing another creature pain. He never did break me, but he did his darnedest." Ware's voice softened. "He did at that."

"I'm sorry. That sounds awful." Erin ventured a glance at him. "I've had a lot of different parents, and some of them… they think if they hurt you bad enough… I don't know if they really think you'll change, or if it just makes them feel better." She shook her head. She tried to see the boy this old man had once been. The little boy who had not wanted to hurt any living thing and was beaten mercilessly by a father who felt that he had to if they were going to survive. "I'm sorry he was like that."

Ware gazed back at her, his eyes far away. "I found these caves way back then. Looking for somewhere to shelter. Somewhere I could sleep and be safe. My pirate grotto to run away to, when things got too rough at home."

Minutes of silence ticked by.

"Can you show me where Bella is?" Erin asked.

"You're going to have to go farther."

"Okay. I'll do my best."

"Don't know how long it will be before your friends get reinforcements. They're not going to stay above ground forever."

"I can talk to Terry. We can explain…"

"Nothing to explain. He already knows the lay of the land. He's got a job to do."

Erin didn't know what was going to happen. It wasn't going to be good. She didn't want another case to end with more bodies than there were when she started investigating it. Too many lives had been lost already.

"Where's Bella?"

Ware escorted her through the tunnels. She tried to trust that he knew where it was safe and where the dangerous places were. She had to trust that he wasn't just going to push her off of a ledge or let her walk out into nothingness. The flashlight wasn't strong enough for her to be confident of her footing.

Everything he had told her could have been a lie. Some people lied compulsively. Without even knowing why, they told story after story just plucked from the air.

For all she knew, he could be a mass murderer. And still she felt sorry for him.

The cave system had been getting cooler and cooler the farther they went into it. Erin was past goosebumps into full-blown shivering. Ware was dressed for the cave, with a long-sleeved flannel shirt and long pants, thick and sturdy.

Then they stepped into a cave that radiated warmth. Erin's mind jumped illogically to volcanoes and lava and the center of the earth. Had they gone so far that they had reached a source of natural heat?

But as she looked around, she saw that wasn't the case. There was a fire. Built where there had obviously been a lot of fires before it. There was lots of white ash on the rock floor and the cave walls were coated with black soot. Up above, there was a natural chimney that drew the smoke out, so cave didn't just fill with smoke to smother them all.

Erin saw a shape beside the fire. A full figure and mop of curly blond hair that she recognized. Erin moved forward of her own accord for the first time.

"Bella! Bella, are you okay?"

Bella stirred and looked at Erin. Her eyes were distant, and it took her a few minutes to focus in on Erin. She pushed herself up. She was tied up, but still had some freedom of movement and didn't seem particularly aware of her situation.

"Erin?" Her voice was vague and uncertain. "What are you doing here?"

"Are you okay? Did he do anything to hurt you?"

"I'm fine."

COUP DE GLACE

But there was clearly something wrong with her. Had she gotten too cold? Not been able to get the oxygen she needed? Erin took in a deep breath, but the air in the cave smelled fresh, not stale.

"They're going to come for us," Erin told Bella, squeezing one of her hands. "They know where we are, and they're going to come and get us."

"Okay," Bella agreed.

"You're not hurt?"

"No. But you are. What happened?"

"I... fell..."

Erin looked at Ware. The angry man was gone. The man who had teased and joked with Bella was gone. Even the little boy who had been beaten for refusing to hunt for the family was gone. He just seemed like an empty shell. Like a meringue egg, which, broken open, turned out to be empty.

"Why did you bring us here?"

"This is where I used to come," Ware said, turning in a slow circle to look around the chamber. "Before I was worried about finding any gold or minerals in here. Before... when the only thing I wanted was somewhere warm and sheltered, where I was safe."

"So this was your pirate grotto."

"Yes," Ware agreed tiredly. "This is where it all began."

They were all quiet for a while. Erin strained her ears for some sign of Terry or the others. As Ware had said, sooner or later they would descend into the caves to find her and Bella. They would bring their guns. They would arrest Ware, assuming they could talk him into putting down his little cannon. If not, his pirate's grotto would be the site of his last stand.

Erin felt like she needed to keep Ware talking, if only to cover up the sounds of their rescuers' approach for as long as possible. To give them a way to find the shelter among all of the labyrinthine passageways. Erin would never forgive herself if something happened to one of the rescuers because they got lost in the tunnels.

"Mr. Ware..."

"Maybe you could call me Grandpa," Ware said. "That's what the little girl has been calling me."

It was funny for him to call Bella little, but Erin supposed that Ware's years gave him the right to think of her as just a tot if he wanted to. And if it meant he wouldn't hurt them, she didn't care what he wanted them to call him.

"Okay... Grandpa..."

"That's nice. I don't have any granddaughters of my own, and I always felt like I missed out because of it."

"What happened to Grandma Prost? You buried her beside Ezekiel, didn't you?"

He stared into the fire. "It was a long time ago, now. Sometimes it's just best to let things be."

"Some things need closure. The townspeople thought that it was Ezekiel. That he had gone crazy and killed her. Or that he had found her dead and buried her himself. For twenty years, people have blamed him for it."

"He didn't go crazy. Not until after she died."

"So do you know what happened? Can you tell me?"

"It was that darn fence... why did he have to be so stubborn about it? Why did he have to say no? I told him I'd swap with him. Hills and trees he couldn't do anything with for flat pasture he could use. Why would he say no to that? It was a good deal for him. He wasn't losing anything. He would get good pasture land out of it."

"Why did he say no?"

"Because of the cemetery... the title for this land includes the cemetery, and it includes caveats that the land can't be developed or subdivided, so that the cemetery will always be protected. I told him I'd take care of it. I wouldn't develop it. I wouldn't try to move it or develop it. I just... wanted the caves."

"Did he know that was what you wanted? And why?"

"Of course not. I would never tell him that. I learned from my Pappy to keep my mouth shut and not act like a sissy."

"And when he said no to the land swap, you tried moving the fence line."

"Not to where it is now. Just... a little at a time. So that he'd never know what I was doing..."

"Except he did."

"He had eyes like an eagle. Even though I only moved it a foot, a few inches, he knew it as soon as he saw it. He knew it, and he made such a big fuss about it that everybody else knew it too." He was silent for a time. "Martha was up here tending to the graves. She was always such a great gardener."

She didn't die tending the graves. Something had happened.

"When she saw me working on the fence, she guessed I wasn't just repairing it. She came after me, screaming about the property line, that I'd better leave the fence alone and keep to my own property. She said that when Ezekiel was upset, he'd take it out on her, even though it wasn't her he was angry with." He swallowed. "If she'd been my wife, I would never have done anything to hurt her!"

Erin looked at Bella to see if she was taking in all that Mr. Ware said. But Bella didn't seem to understand what was going on or being said. She dozed by the fire, giving no indication of being interested in the conversation. This was the revelation she was looking for, what she had asked Erin to find out for her, but she was too dopey to understand it.

"What happened?"

"She tried to wrestle my tools away from me. What did it matter? I could come back later. I could buy new tools. There wasn't any point in fighting over them."

"But you did. You didn't know what was going to happen."

"No. I was just reacting to her trying to take something that was mine. They wouldn't let me have the caves. She tried to take away my tools. Threatened to call in the sheriff and have me arrested. I just wanted what was rightfully mine!"

But discovering the caves and making them his boyhood refuge didn't make them his. He was trying to steal them, just as surely as Martha had tried to take away his tools.

"I pushed her away and she fell." Ware shook his head bleakly.

Erin tried to picture it. What had happened? Had she hit her head? Had a heart attack?

The cave was full of paraphernalia that had built up there over the years. Things that he had brought as a boy to make it more comfortable. Precious possessions he had perhaps wanted to hide from an abusive father. Tools that he had used for mining those first years, hand tools that must have taken weeks to get results that would have been instantaneous with power tools or explosives. Ware was staring at a basket of tools. At first, they didn't look any different from the rest of the tools littering the room. But then Erin realized it was a basket of gardening tools.

Grandma Prost had been tending to the graves. Digging and edging and using the long shears to clip the grass around the headstones. Long, sharp blades. If she fell while holding the shears or the basket of tools, she could have been badly injured. Out in the wilds, away from any help, far from hospitals and medical care, there might have been nothing Ware could do for her.

"You never meant to hurt any living thing," Erin said softly.

"My pappy thought I was a coward. Maybe he was right. Maybe there is something wrong with my head. He said it's only natural, taking a life to preserve your own." He shook his head, eyes glistening. "You couldn't expect me to tell anyone. Ezekiel would kill me. They would put me in prison. I'd never survive there. Not a... a *pacifist* like me."

"It was an accident. Maybe you wouldn't have had to go to prison."

"Things were different those days. You don't know what it was like. They would have killed me."

Erin couldn't think of what else to say.

Chapter Twenty-Three

IT SEEMED LIKE THEY were stuck in the cave for an eternity. It wasn't like it had been the last time. Erin was hurt, but only superficially. She wasn't lying alone in the dark wondering if she was going to be able to survive. She knew that Terry would come. It would take time to get reinforcements and to devise a plan, but he would come back for her. It was important not to agitate Ware. She couldn't know what he was capable of if he got worked up. He said that Martha Prost's death had been an accident, but that might just be how he chose to color it twenty years later.

He might be a pacifist, incapable of harming another living soul by choice, or he might be dangerous, lying to cover up a cold-blooded killing for profit. He couldn't deny that he had a gun and that he had held it on her, threatening her. He'd grabbed her and pushed her around. He'd already made her hurt herself once, no matter how innocent he claimed to be.

The fire made Erin drowsy once the adrenaline started to seep away. She shivered at first, all of her muscles quivering, and then the shakiness was replaced by the overwhelming desire to just curl up and go to sleep. Ware withdrew into himself, not talking to her, holding the gun in his lap and staring at it. He moaned and he whispered to himself, a man who had been alone with his own company for many years.

COUP DE GLACE

Erin cuddled up to Bella, trying to protect her and to reassure herself that everything was okay. She closed her eyes, drifting in the suffocating warmth of the fire.

She awoke with a start, hearing them coming. In the quiet of the caves, sound carried. As stealthy as they tried to be, the men couldn't completely mask the sounds of their footsteps and their words with each other as they coordinated the search through the caves. Erin sat up, trying to force alertness. She had to protect herself and Bella in whatever was to come. Bella was even dopier than Erin was, and she thought it more than just the warmth of the room. Maybe Ware had given her something to keep her quiet. Bella hadn't answered the calls of the searchers, who had been at least as close as the cemetery. Maybe their voices hadn't penetrated that far, or maybe she had heard them but been unable to answer.

"Mr. Ware!"

Erin recognized Terry's voice. She couldn't see him, but his sudden call made Erin jump, startled.

"I want you to put down the gun and come out with your hands behind your head."

Ware looked up from the gun in his lap, eyes unfocused. He made no move to obey.

"Please, Grandpa," Erin said to him. "Listen to what they say. Do what they say, and you'll be okay."

He looked in her direction. "Grandpa. I like that."

"You would have made a good grandpa. It's too bad you didn't have any grandchildren."

"I never even had a sweetheart," he said sadly. "Last in my line, and not even fit to marry."

"Couldn't you have found a girl like you, who respected your values?"

"A man had to be able to provide for his family. How could I have done that? I was worthless. Worse than worthless, needing to be fed by the efforts of others. Consuming but never giving anything back."

Erin turned her head slowly, trying to catch a glimpse of Terry. Wherever he was, she couldn't see him.

"Since you aren't going to shoot anyone," she said in a little louder voice, "why don't you just put the gun down?"

"This gun has been in the family for generations. Generations of Wares who have protected their homes and killed for their families. This country was built by guns like this." His voice was loud, as if he were trying to make it sound like he meant what he said, but it was flat and unconvincing.

"But you've never fired it, have you? Does it even work?"

He fiddled with the gun. Erin swallowed. Even if he hadn't ever fired it, that didn't mean they were safe. People got killed all the time by someone who didn't know how to handle a gun. Weapons that weren't supposed to be loaded and were just being handled casually. She was pretty sure that the police weren't going to take Erin's word for it that Ware wouldn't shoot them, or his hostages, or himself. Erin herself couldn't be sure that what he said was true.

"Mr. Ware," Terry's voice came again, loud and firm and in control of the situation. "Put the gun down on the floor in front of you."

Ware didn't move.

"Please, Grandpa," Erin coaxed. "Put it down or give it to me. I'll look after it for you. I don't want you to get hurt."

He looked across the dimly-lit cave at her. "I never meant for that woman to die."

"No. It was an accident. You couldn't have predicted what was going to happen. You hadn't planned to hurt her."

"She was trying to take away my home."

Erin ran her eyes around the walls of the cave. Mr. Ware had lived in the family home since he was born, as far as she knew. He'd probably been completely alone there for twenty to forty years, depending on when his parents had died. But the place he was attached to and considered his home was not the house, but the sanctuary he had discovered as a child. Adverse possession said that a squatter had to occupy the land he claimed for twenty years, but Erin doubted that the law would extend to an underground cave, even if Mr. Ware had used it since childhood.

"I know, Grandpa."

"The little girl… she was there, in the graveyard. She saw the extra grave. She knew what it meant."

Erin nodded. She pictured Bella putting the necklace over the headstone, marking the place where she now knew her grandmother was buried as well. "And she knew something was different. That the fence had been moved from where it was when she was little."

Too close to his secrets.

"I couldn't let her take it away. I told her… I'd show her…"

"And you brought her in here." Erin looked at Bella sleeping by the fire. Had he tied her up before or after bringing her inside? Had she been able to put up a fight? Or had he taken her off guard?

"And the car? How did it get back to the house?"

"I drove it." He shrugged, as if that were obvious. It was a bold move; Cindy could have seen him driving it back or getting out of it at the house. It was in sight of the front door. The dog might have gone after him, or at least sounded the alarm. But he'd gotten cleanly away, so they wouldn't know where Bella had disappeared from. He was a neighbor, so maybe the dog knew him and didn't consider him a threat.

"It's time for us to go," Erin told him. She pushed herself to her feet and stood there for a moment, waiting for her head rush to settle. Her mouth and face still throbbed, but she felt curiously removed from herself. She didn't look in the direction of the cave entrance, where she knew Terry was watching for his opportunity. She walked up to Mr. Ware. "Give that to me now," she told him firmly.

At first, he didn't respond to her any more than he had obeyed Terry's commands, but then he raised his eyes to her, frowning.

"Come on," Erin insisted. "You're not going to shoot me, so just give it to me before someone gets hurt. We don't want any accidents."

Mr. Ware turned the gun around and held it out to her, grip first. Erin hated to touch the weapon, but she swallowed her aversion and took it from him.

"Thank you."

She turned toward the entrance to show Terry that she had it. He emerged from the shelter of the tunnel where he was hidden by the darkness, giving low instructions to someone behind him. He held his gun in front of him, outstretched, pointing directly at Mr. Ware.

"Step back, Erin. As far away from him as you can."

Erin shuffled back away from Mr. Ware, her heart pounding again. The big gun was heavy in her hand, and she held it down at her side, worried about the possibility of triggering it accidentally. Vic and Willie had both suggested that she get firearms training and at least keep a gun in the house, but she was too afraid of accidents. She wished she'd humored them and at least held one before. Then maybe it wouldn't feel so awkward and menacing in her hand.

Terry gave Mr. Ware instructions, pointing the gun at him in a two-handed stance. His voice was sharp, but he wasn't yelling. Not like some of the cops on TV, always screaming and rushing suspects, trying to be as intimidating as possible. When he had Mr. Ware face-down on the rocky floor, he first patted his pockets and body for a hidden weapon before finally holstering his own gun and doing a thorough pat-down. He arrested Ware with a long litany of charges and the usual spiel about his rights. Others came

COUP DE GLACE

into the cave, which quickly became crowded with bodies. The sheriff and Tom. K9 was already with Terry, whining and watching the suspect closely in case he became a threat. Willie was there. He was the one who took the gun from Erin's hand and passed it to the sheriff.

"Are you okay, Erin? You're bleeding."

Erin touched her face and drew it back slippery with blood, almost black in the firelight. "It's fine. I'm okay. Check Bella, he might have given her something."

Willie gave her arm a comforting squeeze and moved on to check out Bella.

After securing Mr. Ware, Terry passed him on to Tom with instructions, then turned to Erin. He enveloped her in a big hug, holding her close against his warm body. "Erin, I was so scared. I'm sorry. I'm so sorry I let him hurt you and bring you down here. I wanted so badly to help you, but I didn't want to escalate him. I needed to get Cindy out of there and to give him a chance to calm down…"

"I know, I know," Erin assured him while the words flowed out in a torrent. "I know. And we needed to find Bella. All of these tunnels… we might not have found her in time if he hadn't brought me here to her."

She remembered her own ordeal, lying hurt and alone in the pitch black, afraid that no one would ever find her. A shudder went through her. Terry felt it and squeezed her more tightly.

"It's okay, Erin. It's all over. You're safe. And Bella is going to be okay. Nobody else got hurt."

"I know." Tears were running down Erin's cheeks. She didn't know why. She hadn't cried while Ware had been holding her. She didn't cry until she was rescued, and then there she was, bawling like a baby.

Terry just kept holding her, rocking back and forth, waiting for her to calm down. "You're probably in shock. We need to get you out of here."

"I can walk." She didn't want to be taken out of there on a stretcher. Not again. She wanted to be able to get out under her own steam, her hands and feet free.

"Let's go, then. Come on."

With a supportive arm around her, he led her to the tunnel she and Ware had entered through. Erin hung onto him, glad to have something to hold on to.

"What if we can't find our way out? What if we get lost?"

"Do you think Willie would let us get lost? Do you think he let me just run in here following your voice and get all turned around? He's too much of a professional for that. I call him in as a consultant, and then he takes charge and I have to listen to what he tells me!"

Erin couldn't help but laugh at his aggrieved tone. "You did the right thing," she assured him. "I'm glad you didn't get lost."

She saw that there were small glow sticks dropped at regular intervals, guiding their way all the way back to the entrance.

Cindy was waiting with other townspeople outside. She pulled away from Lottie, almost tackling Erin in her anxiety. "Where is Bella? Was she in there? Is she okay? They won't let me go in!"

Erin tried to pat Cindy's arm comfortingly. "She's there. She's alive. They'll bring her out in just a minute."

Cindy collapsed. Erin could do nothing to catch her, but Lottie was there and another of the ladies from the town, and they kept her from landing on the ground.

"It's okay, Cind. She's okay," Lottie repeated. "Just hang on. She'll be right out."

"My baby. My baby girl..."

Her earlier fortitude and her anger at Mr. Ware were gone. Just like Erin breaking down once she knew she was safe, Cindy finally gave herself permission to express her anguish over Bella's disappearance. She cried and wailed, her friends doing the best they could to comfort her.

Terry led Erin away from them. He took her to a quiet patch of grass where they sat down and took a breath.

"Did he tell you anything?" he asked. "Why he took Bella and what happened to her grandma?"

Erin nodded and told him about Mr. Ware's emotional claim on the caves and the confrontation with Martha Prost that had led to her accidental death. She told him about the gardening tools in the cave, and he said he'd look after them later.

"We'll need to have a look at everything in that cave. There may be more to the story than he is telling us."

Erin nodded. The feeling she'd had that Ware might not be telling her the full story was validated by Terry's words. "I don't know exactly what happened, but at least we know one thing—it wasn't Ezekiel Prost who killed his wife. He's been blamed for it all these years, but it wasn't him."

They turned toward the cave entrance as a hush fell over the group gathered in the glade. Willie came out first, turned around backward. He was holding on to Bella's arms and helped to pull her up. She leaned on him for support and looked around in a daze. Cindy fell on her, crying and cuddling her daughter to her. Willie hovered close by, hands out to catch Bella, but Cindy held on tightly and didn't let her go.

"She's dehydrated," Willie said. "I don't think she's had anything to drink since she disappeared, and she's been lying by the fire. Give her some water, and we should probably get her to the hospital where they can put her on an IV for a few hours."

Erin watched the ministrations over Bella, grateful that she wasn't the one who had been languishing underground this time. She'd only been there for a few hours and didn't need to go to the hospital. Terry got back to his feet to talk to Cindy about interviewing Bella as soon as she was settled at the hospital.

"I don't want you talking to her about it," he warned. "Don't ask questions and taint her memories. Just be supportive. Leave the questioning to me."

Cindy nodded. She and her friends walked Bella back toward the car so they could take her to the hospital. Bella walked slowly but seemed to be unharmed.

"How about you?" Willie asked Erin. "Are you okay?"

Erin dabbed at her sore mouth. "I'll be fine. Thanks for coming to our rescue—again."

"Any time you get stuck underground, you can expect me to come looking for you." Willie looked around and motioned to someone in the crowd. It wasn't until then that Erin saw Vic.

"Oh, Vicky! Come on over. It's okay," Erin told her.

Vic separated from the crowd and hurried over to Erin. She sat down beside Erin and gave her a hug around the shoulders. "You gotta stop doing this," she said. "It just kills me to stand around waiting for someone to find you and bring you up."

"It wasn't planned," Erin assured her. "I didn't come here to go caving."

"Spelunking," Vic corrected, smiling because she knew Erin had said it just to tease her.

"Spelunking. I just came to look at the graveyard again. I had no plans to go into any cave."

"But it doesn't seem to stop you." Vic shook her head. "Now y'all been down in that cave and I haven't! Is it at least a good one?"

Erin rolled her eyes. She turned her head to get Willie's opinion. "It's big, lots bigger than you'd ever guess by the entrance. I don't know how many tunnels there are; Mr. Ware said they run all over Tennessee."

"That's an exaggeration," Willie said with a wry smile. "But there are definitely a few miles of passages."

"And Mr. Ware said there was gold," Erin said, keeping her voice very low so that the other spectators nearby wouldn't overhear her. "He said that was pretty rare in these parts."

"Almost unheard of," Willie agreed. "In fact, I'd be surprised if it was true." He cracked open a water bottle and took a sip, then offered it to Erin. "Just don't get blood in it."

"You don't think there's any gold?" Erin asked.

"Probably not. I don't see any sign of a vein or that he's been moving any ore out of there. If he was doing any actual mining, there would be rock to be taken out. But you'd have trouble even getting a small wheelbarrow through that opening, let alone anything that could move large amounts of rock."

"There could be another entrance, something where it's easier to get out."

"Could be. But I didn't see any indication of any real work going on. Or any mineral deposits that would lead me to think there was gold in there. Or anything else valuable."

"Just his memories," Erin decided. "He said he found it when he was a little boy. It's where he used to go to escape his father."

Willie nodded. "That, I can believe. Most miners don't actually have any desire to live underground, but he had a lot of personal stuff down there. Mementos. Things to make him more comfortable. It makes sense that it was sort of his private clubhouse."

"A refuge."

"Well... his daddy died a long time ago. Time for him to face life."

"I hope he *isn't* facing life," Erin said, twisting the meaning of his words. "If Martha Prost died by accident... then what sentence is he looking at? For kidnapping and whatever else...?"

"I'm not the expert. Terry might have an idea, but neither of us is a lawyer."

Willie motioned for Terry to join them to talk. Terry looked at his watch, then walked back over. "I have to head over to the hospital before too long. Sheriff and Tom can take care of the scene. What's up?"

"Just wondering what kind of time Ware is looking at. What is he being charged with?"

"Two kidnappings, weapons charges, resisting, maybe Mrs. Prost's murder. He'll probably spend the rest of his life behind bars. Don't know if he'll actually make it to trial or not. He's not a young man and jail conditions are not exactly conducive to good health."

"He's afraid of how he'll be treated by the other prisoners," Erin told him.

"He's not a child molester or murderer, so he won't be segregated. I doubt if anyone will really care about an old man who's not associated with any cartels or gangs. They have more important things to worry about."

"So you think he'll be left alone?"

Terry looked at her and couldn't come up with an answer. Eventually, he just shook his head. He looked at his watch again and said he needed to get to the hospital.

"I'll catch up with you tonight, okay? You'll be okay? I can get your statement tonight or tomorrow, you don't need to hang around here."

"Okay," Erin said with a nod of relief. "I think I'd just like to go home and relax for the rest of the day."

"Go ahead. You deserve it. Especially after the way you handled Mr. Ware and got him to give you his gun. I was really worried about gunfire and hostages in an enclosed chamber. It could have turned out very differently."

"Was it loaded? He said he'd never used it."

"It was loaded," Willie said. "But I believe the part about him never having used it before."

COUP DE GLACE

"Why? Was it... loaded the wrong way?" Erin asked uncertainly.

Willie smiled. "No firing pin. He couldn't have shot anything if he'd wanted to."

Chapter Twenty-Four

REG WAS HOME WHEN Erin got there. She seemed surprised to see Erin and Vic.

"I thought you'd be at the bakery. What are you doing home already?"

"Things have been a little crazy today," Erin said, shaking her head. "Didn't your powers of divination tell you that?"

"My…?" She actually looked at Erin. "Holy heck. What happened to you? You didn't have a fight with that boyfriend of yours, did you? Cops always think they can get away with it, especially in small towns like this. Don't you put up with it!"

"It wasn't Terry! That's two strikes," Vic said in delight. "One more, and you're out. I thought you were so good at reading people."

"It's different with Erin," Reg excused herself. "She's known me for so long, she can block me. And I wasn't ready to do a cold reading. I just got up from a nap, and I haven't had a chance to get my motor running yet…"

"Erin has been busy catching Martha Prost's murderer. You know, the ghost you talked to?"

"Really?" Reg's eyes got big. "You solved the ghost case? I'll bet she was somewhere cold, wasn't she? I've been getting chills all afternoon, I knew something was happening on the case… You should have taken me with you. I could have helped you to figure it out faster."

COUP DE GLACE

Erin rolled her eyes. She remembered when Reg had been the big sister, someone Erin looked up to, so much more sophisticated and knowledgeable than Erin. Reg had known everything, and Erin had idolized her. Wanted to do everything like her. How many stupid schemes had she participated in and how many times had she gotten in trouble, because she'd been stupid enough to buy into Reg's nonsense?

Reg was still stuck in the same place, still trying to scheme and talk her way into wealth or a reputation, but Erin had grown up.

Erin gave her a little smile, though it made her cut lip crack again, causing a flash of pain.

"It's all done, now, Reg. You missed out on it."

"You should have called me," Reg complained. "You should have let me come with you. If it was me, I would have included you."

"Have you found somewhere else to stay yet?" Erin changed the subject. "You said you'd have somewhere inside a week."

Reg looked uncomfortable. "I didn't count on how small this town is. No one has anything."

"Maybe you'd better find another town, then," Erin said unsympathetically. "You've about worn out my hospitality."

Reg looked at her sullenly, then shrugged. "Fine. I'll get out of your way. Tomorrow."

"Thanks. Sorry things didn't work out for you here."

Reg stared at Erin for a few long moments. "You've changed," she said finally. "I thought you were still the same old Erin underneath all of this professional baker stuff. But you're different."

"It's called growing up. Finding your place in the world. What is it you actually want to do with your life, Reg? You want to keep acting like a carnival fortune teller? Or is there something else you'd actually like to do with your life?"

"I don't know, but I can tell you I don't want to be tied down to a place like this. If I had inherited the bakery and this house, you can bet I would have liquidated it. I wouldn't be tied to all of this."

Erin nodded and didn't argue. They were two different people, and while she hadn't thought she'd ever have the opportunity to settle down with her own home and her own business, she'd been quick to do it when the chance came along. Reg wouldn't have taken the opportunity. She would have just tried to get whatever money she could have out of it and blown it all on some new scam.

"Well, good luck with whatever is next. Me... I'm going to take a nap."

Erin said her goodbyes to Vic and Reg and retired to her room.

Orange Blossom had obviously been sleeping in Reg's room, but when he heard Erin going to her bed, he jumped down from Reg's bed and hurried after Erin, yowling inquiringly after her, confused by her strange behavior. Erin rarely had time for a midday nap and, even when she did, she rarely took it. There was too much to do. Too much planning. Too many lists. Too many frozen treats to be made.

"Come on, then," Erin told the cat. "Come and get some cuddles."

Soon, he was curled up under her chin, his whole body vibrating with purrs. Erin closed her eyes and went to sleep.

Monday everything was back to normal, with Erin and Vic at the bakery early, baking the day's bread and then opening to the usual morning crowd.

What wasn't usual was that Bella was there even though it wasn't her shift. Erin had watched her drive up to the bakery in her mother's car, but with Cindy nowhere in sight. Bella was driving herself.

COUP DE GLACE

She came in and ordered a cookie and tea just like any other regular customer. Erin sensed something different in her. A new determination and independence. Far from withdrawing into herself after the horror of the kidnapping, she had instead remade herself. She was the new and improved Bella, confident and unafraid.

"You look really good," Erin told her. "No one would guess that just two days ago…"

"I'm not even going to talk about it," Bella said, holding her hands up. "Yesterday is over and today is a new day with new opportunities. I'm not going to waste another day fussing and worrying about things that are outside my control."

"Good for you. I don't know if I could ever stop myself from worrying. But I agree about taking on every new day… like a gift. Who knows what tomorrow will bring. Just deal with one day at a time."

"What good did worrying ever do for anyone? I spent my whole life worrying about what my mother would think, what the people in the town would think, what the right thing to do was… but I'm done that now."

Erin considered this. "Your mom loves you."

"I know that. But I'm not a little kid anymore. I can't just stay there my whole life, sheltered by her. She shouldn't have stayed there all this time. She should have gone to the city or somewhere she could be her own person. Like she was before Grandma disappeared."

"You think she should have sold the farm and done something else?"

"She's never been happy here. I don't know about selling the farm. Maybe someone else could stay here and look after it until she was ready to retire. But she hates it here. She should have gone on to do what she wanted."

Erin nodded. She didn't know Cindy Prost well, but the woman had never seemed particularly happy. If she'd left a happy, independent life to look after her father and then her daughter, her resentment was understandable.

The bells over the door jingled, and she and Bella looked up to see who it was. Reg stood in the doorway for a moment, looking first behind the counter where Vic was, then at the table where Erin stood talking to Bella.

"Oh, there you are. I just came to tell you… I'm heading out. I guess this is it."

"You can call me," Erin said. "Keep in touch. I'd like to know how you're getting on."

"As long as I'm not living here."

"I don't think it was a good fit," Erin said, keeping the comment as neutral as possible.

Reg swept back her hair. "No, I thought a little backwater town would be a good place to set up shop. Lots of superstitious people, don't get out much, they could use some entertainment." She shrugged. "But it wasn't like I thought it would be."

"Is that all this was to you?" Bella demanded. "Entertainment?"

Reg looked at her. "I tried to help you," she said. "That wasn't fake. I never said I'd be able to solve your Grandma's murder… but in the end, it did get solved."

"By Erin, not by you."

"I didn't say I did. But I did communicate with her. Maybe that helped Erin to figure out what was going on." Reg gave a shrug. "You never know how these things are meant to unfold. What we call coincidence and intuition…"

Bella gave her a scornful look. "You said that she was cold where she was and that she wanted to be buried next to my grandpa."

"Yes. That's what she communicated to me."

"But she *was* buried next to my grandpa."

"Err…" Reg looked for an answer. Then she looked at her phone, feigning surprise. "Is it that late? I'd better be getting on my way."

COUP DE GLACE

She stepped closer to Erin, gave her a hug and an air kiss, resting her cheek against Erin's for an instant, then pulled away.

"I'll write," she promised. "Or something."

Chapter Twenty-Five

ERIN WAS CLEANING UP when her phone rang. She had a good idea who it would be and pulled it out of her apron pocket.

"Hi, Terry."

"Are you okay to get together for a while this evening, or are you too tired?"

"Either way, I need to eat." Erin wouldn't really be sure how she felt until she'd had a chance to sit down and relax. Then it might all catch up with her.

"Do you mind eating at home today? Would that be too much work? We can just have sandwiches."

"That's fine. Why don't you pick up a packaged salad at the grocery store? I'm not sure what's in the fridge."

"Okay. I'll see you in half an hour or so."

Erin ended the call and slid the phone back into her pocket. "Terry's coming over. You want to join us?"

Vic shook her head. "Willie and I already have plans. You guys can have the house to yourselves." She winked. "Don't do anything I wouldn't do."

Erin felt herself blushing for no reason. Rather than protesting, she tried to raise her eyebrow in an enigmatic quirk, but wasn't sure whether she succeeded or just ended up making one of the crazy faces she and Reg used to practice on each other.

It was obvious when she let Terry in at the house an hour later that he had something on his mind. He took the salad into the kitchen to put it in a bowl and mix it, but said barely a word to her. Erin started to get the sandwich fixings out.

"What's up?"

"What makes you think something is up?"

"I may not be a detective, but I think I can tell when something is wrong." She studied him. "Is it work? Something go off the rails with Mr. Ware?" She remembered how he had said he wouldn't last in prison and hoped something hadn't already happened to him. Surely, they would be careful when introducing a new prisoner into the general population.

Terry's dimple was nowhere to be seen. His lips were pressed tightly together and there was a frown line between his brows. K9 watched him, panting.

"It's not Mr. Ware."

"But it is work? I guess it's not something you can talk to me about?"

He seemed to be torn. Erin lifted her hands in a questioning gesture.

"It's about Reg."

"Reg is gone. You don't need to worry about her anymore. I told her she'd been imposing on my hospitality long enough and sent her on her way."

"Did she say where she was going?"

"No. I asked her to keep in touch… but it could be another ten years before she decides to talk to me again. She's like that."

"No idea where she might go? Any mutual friend who might be able to put you into contact with her?"

"Uh… I don't know." Erin thought through their various acquaintances. Was there anyone Reg might keep in closer contact with? "What's wrong?"

"Your sister made off with several family heirlooms when she left town."

Erin's stomach clenched. She turned away from the table, where she had been laying down plates. "No! Oh, tell me she didn't!"

Terry didn't recant. Erin had known he wouldn't. He wouldn't have joked about something like that. And it wasn't something Erin would have put past Reg. Erin reached for the nearest chair and sat down with a thump, her knees weak.

"Oh, Terry, I'm so sorry. Who? What did she take?"

"I can't give you a list, those reports are confidential. But I did get reports from several women that are remarkably consistent with each other."

"What did she do? Did she steal from their houses? I said she was trouble. I knew this wasn't going to turn out well!"

"She apparently would ask for an item that the dearly departed would have valued, for her to hold on to and get a clearer picture of the person they wanted to talk to. She asked to hold on to them for a day or two, so she could really get to know them, and then set up appointments to return the valuables and give a reading. But when word spread that she'd left town... we started to get anxious calls."

"Oh, Regina," Erin groaned.

"Do you mind if I check her room, just to make sure she didn't leave anything here?"

"You don't think she'd leave heirloom jewelry here."

"No. I'm hoping maybe a note scribbled on the bedside table, a reservation number, something that might indicate what direction she was going."

"Of course. You know which room she was in. The one that used to be Vic's."

"I thought you were going to take back the master bedroom after Vic left."

Erin shrugged. "Mine is too cozy. I can't bring myself to take Clementine's room."

COUP DE GLACE

Piper clicked his tongue at K9 and went to search Clementine's bedroom. Erin hadn't yet had a chance to see what needed to be tidied away and to change the sheets; everything was just as Reg had left it. Terry was back a couple of minutes later shaking his head.

"Nothing there. In fact, you might want to check and make sure she didn't abscond with any of your valuables."

She shook her head. "No… if she had the nerve to steal from me… I don't want to know about it. I really don't."

They turned their attention to their supper, both quiet and pondering over the developments individually. Orange Blossom was under foot, while K9 stayed politely by Terry's chair and Marshmallow kept to the side of the room, watching them all with one eye.

They avoided any further discussion of Reg during dinner, instead talking about the weather, their friends, and the bakery, occasionally returning to the subject of Mr. Ware and Martha Prost.

"Bella even went downstairs to the storeroom today," Erin told him after they had adjourned to the living room couch. "She hasn't gone down the hall to the commode yet, but she went downstairs, and that's a huge improvement. I wouldn't be surprised if she actually made it to the loo one of these days."

"She's a brave girl," Terry said. "I don't think she knew that about herself before."

Erin nodded. "She's spent too much time worrying about ghosts and being safe from things that were never really a threat. I think this experience… forced her to see that there are a lot worse things in life. There's no point spending your time worrying about things that don't really matter."

"A good lesson," Terry agreed pointedly.

"I don't spend a lot of time worrying. And I'm not afraid of ghosts."

"I still think you worry more than you need to. And like Bella... you worry about what other people are saying about you."

"I'm going to try not to."

The doorbell rang. Erin looked at the clock on the wall. K9 lifted his head and looked in the direction of the door, his ears pricked curiously, but he didn't give any sign that there was danger lurking outside.

Erin went to the door. She flicked on the outside light and looked out the peephole. She didn't have the burglar alarm armed like Terry thought she should in the evening, but she couldn't be much safer, at home with the town cop. She opened the door.

"Charley, hi! Come on in."

Charley entered. She saw Terry on the couch and gave a sly smile. "Well, I'll be sure not to interrupt you for too long."

"Come visit with us for a few minutes."

Charley sat down in an easy chair, and Erin slid back into the warm spot next to Terry. He put his arm around her.

"I just got word from the estate lawyers," Charley said, leaning forward excitedly. "They've finally agreed to let me open The Bake Shoppe!"

Erin's stomach tightened into a knot. "They did? That's great news for you. Does that mean..." She frowned, trying to sort it out. "They've decided to give you Davis's portion as well?"

"Not yet. They're going to hold half of the estate in trust, but for now, they're letting me control the decisions about what to do with the bakery. They said that since Davis hasn't been proven guilty of causing Trenton's death, they can't take his portion away from him yet. If he's found guilty, they will. Until then, they're just going to hold it."

Erin nodded. "Well... I'm glad it's working out for you. I guess that means we'll both be in the baking business."

COUP DE GLACE

Erin's job was going to be that much more difficult with a direct competitor.

"I'm still not getting up that early in the morning. I'll have other people to do that for me."

Erin laughed. "You're not exactly a morning person."

"No. But…" She made a gesture like she didn't know what to do with her hands. "I wanted to thank you for what you did."

Erin glanced over at Terry. "I just did what anyone would have. There was written evidence that Davis knew about Trenton's allergy and that it could be fatal. There's enough circumstantial evidence piling up to show that he and Joelle knew exactly what they were doing and were happy with the results."

Terry nodded.

"So… thanks for that," Charley said again. "I don't know that it was the smartest business decision for you, but I appreciate it. I'm sure people in town will be happy to have The Bake Shoppe open again. No offense to your baking—you make some amazing stuff—but some people just want traditional wheat breads."

"I'm sure there's enough business for two bakeries." Erin had said it many times before, but had never doubted her own words so much. She gave Charley a reassuring smile she did not feel. "I'm looking forward to it."

Sign up for my mailing list at pdworkman.com and get Gluten-Free Murder for free!

JOIN MY MAILING LIST AND

Download a sweet mystery for free

Preview of She Wore Mourning

Chapter One

Zachary Goldman stared down the telephoto lens at the subjects before him. It was one of those days that left tourists gaping over the gorgeous scenery. Dark trees against crisp white snow, with the mountains as a backdrop. Like the picture on a Christmas card.

The thought made Zachary feel sick.

But he wasn't looking at the scenery. He was looking at the man and the woman in a passionate embrace. The pretty young woman's cheeks were flushed pink, more likely with her excitement than the cold, since she had barely stepped out of her car to greet the man. He had a swarthier complexion and a thin black beard, and was currently turned away from Zachary's camera.

Zachary wasn't much to look at himself. Average height, black hair cut too short, his own three-day growth of beard not hiding how pinched and pale his face was. He'd never considered himself a good catch.

He waited patiently for them to move, to look around at their surroundings so that he could get a good picture of their faces.

They thought they were alone; that no one could see them without being seen. They hadn't counted on the fact that Zachary had been surveilling them for a couple of weeks and had known where they would go. They gave him lots of warning so that he could park his car out of sight, camouflage himself in the trees, and settle in to wait for their appearance. He was no amateur; he'd been a private investigator since she had been choosing wedding dresses for her Barbie dolls.

He held down the shutter button to take a series of shots as they came up for air and looked around at the magnificent surroundings, smiling at each other, eyes shining.

All the while, he was trying to keep the negative thoughts at bay. Why had he fallen into private detection? It was one of the few ways he could make a living using his skill with a camera. He could have chosen another profession. He didn't need to spend his whole life following other people, taking pictures of their most private moments. What was the real point of his job? He destroyed lives, something he'd had his fill of long ago. When was the last time he'd brought a smile to a client's face? A real, genuine smile? He had wanted to make a difference in people's lives; to exonerate the innocent.

Zachary's phone started to buzz in his pocket. He lowered the camera and turned around, walking farther into the grove of trees. He had the pictures he needed. Anything else would be overkill.

He pulled out his phone and looked at it. Not recognizing the number, he swiped the screen to answer the call.

"Goldman Investigations."

"Uh... yes... Is this Mr. Goldman?" a voice inquired. Older, female, with a tentative quaver.

"Yes, this is Zachary," he confirmed, subtly nudging her away from the 'mister.'

"Mr. Goldman, my name is Molly Hildebrandt."

He hoped she wasn't calling her about her sixty-something-year-old husband and his renewed interest in sex. If it was another infidelity case, he was going to have to turn it down for his own sanity. He would even take a lost dog or wedding ring. As long as the ring wasn't on someone else's finger now.

"Mrs. Hildebrandt. How can Goldman Investigations help you?"

Of course, she had probably already guessed that Goldman Investigations consisted of only one employee. Most people seemed to sense that from the size of his advertisements. From the fact that he listed a post office box number instead of a business suite downtown or in one of the newer commercial areas. It wasn't really a secret.

"I don't know whether you have been following the news at all about Declan Bond, the little boy who drowned...?"

Zachary frowned. He trudged back toward his car.

"I'm familiar with the basics," he hedged. A four- or five-year-old boy whose round face and feathery dark hair had been pasted all over the news after a search for a missing child had ended tragically.

"They announced a few weeks ago that it was determined to be an accident."

Zachary ground his teeth. "Yes...?"

"Mr. Goldman, I was Declan's grandma." Her voice cracked. Zachary waited, listening to her sniffles and sobs as she tried to get herself under control. "I'm sorry. This has been very difficult for me. For everyone."

"Yes."

"Mr. Goldman, I don't believe that it was an accident. I'm looking for someone who would investigate the matter privately."

Zachary breathed out. A homicide investigation? Of a child? He'd told himself that he would take anything that wasn't infidelity, but if there was one thing that was more depressing than couples cheating on each other, it was the death of a child.

COUP DE GLACE

"I'm sure there are private investigators that would be more qualified for a homicide case than I am, Mrs. Hildebrandt. My schedule is pretty full right now."

Which, of course, was a lie. He had the usual infidelities, insurance investigations, liabilities, and odd requests. The dregs of the private investigation business. Nothing substantial like a homicide. It was a high-profile case. A lot of volunteers had shown up to help, expecting to find a child who had wandered out of his own yard, expecting to find him dirty and crying, not floating face down in a pond. A lot of people had mourned the death of a child they hadn't even known existed before his disappearance.

"I need your help, Mr. Goldman. Zachary. I can't afford a big name, but you've got good references. You've investigated deaths before. Can't you help me?"

He wondered who she had talked to. It wasn't like there were a lot of people who would give him a bad reference. He was competent and usually got the job done, but he wasn't a big name.

"I could meet with you," he finally conceded. "The first consultation is free. We'll see what kind of a case you have and whether I want to take it. I'm not making any promises at this point. Like I said, my schedule is pretty full already."

She gave a little half-sob. "Thank you. When are you able to come?"

After he had hung up, Zachary climbed into his car, putting his camera down on the floor in front of the passenger seat where it couldn't fall, and started the car. For a while, he sat there, staring out the front windshield at the magical, sparkling, Christmas-card scene. Every year, he told himself it would be better. He would get over it and be able to move on and to enjoy the holiday season like everyone else. Who cared about his crappy childhood experiences? People moved on.

And when he had married Bridget, he had thought he was going to achieve it. They would have a fairy-tale Christmas. They would have hot chocolate after skating at the public rink. They would wander down Main Street looking at the lights and the crèche in front of the church. They would open special, meaningful presents from each other.

But they'd fought over Christmas. Maybe it was Zachary's fault. Maybe he had sabotaged it with his gloom. The season brought with it so much baggage. There had been no skating rink. No hot chocolate, only hot tempers. No walks looking at the lights or the nativity. They had practically thrown their gifts at each other, flouncing off to their respective corners to lick their wounds and pout away the holiday.

He'd still cherished the thought that perhaps the next year there would be a baby. What could be more perfect than Christmas with a baby? It would unite them. Make them a real family. Just like Zachary had longed for since he'd lost his own family. He and Bridget and a baby. Maybe even twins. Their own little family in their own little happy bubble.

But despite a positive pregnancy test, things had gone horribly wrong.

Zachary stared at the bright white scenery and blinked hard, trying to shake off the shadows of the past. The past was past. Over and done. This year he was back to baching it for Christmas. Just him and a beer and *It's a Wonderful Life* on TV.

He put the car in reverse and didn't look into the rear-view mirror as he backed up, even knowing about the precipice behind him. He'd deliberately parked where he'd have to back up toward the cliff when he was done. There was a guardrail, but if he backed up too quickly, the car would go right through it, and who could say whether it had been accidental or deliberate? He had been cold-stone sober and had been out on a job. Mrs. Hildebrandt could testify that he had been calm and sober during their call. It would be ruled an accident.

But his bumper didn't even touch the guardrail before he shifted into drive and pulled forward onto the road.

He'd meet with the grandmother. Then, assuming he did not take the case, there would always be another opportunity.

Life was full of opportunities.

~ ~ ~

She Wore Mourning is the first book in the Zachary Goldman Mysteries series.

About the Author

For as long as P.D. Workman can remember, the blank page has held an incredible allure. After a number of false starts, she finally wrote her first complete novel at the age of twelve. It was full of fantastic ideas. It was the springboard for many stories over the next few years. Then, forty-some novels later, P.D. Workman finally decided to start publishing. Lots more are on the way!

P.D. Workman is a devout wife and a mother of one, born and raised in Alberta, Canada. She is a homeschooler and an Executive Assistant. She has a passion for art and nature, creative cooking for special diets, and running. She loves to read, to listen to audio books, and to share books out loud with her family. She is a technology geek with a love for all kinds of gadgets and tools to make her writing and work easier and more fun. In person, she is far less well-spoken than on the written page and tends to be shy and reserved with all but those closest to her.

~ ~ ~

Please visit P.D. Workman at pdworkman.com to see what else she is working on, to join her mailing list, and to link to her social networks.

~ ~ ~

If you enjoyed this book, please take the time to recommend it to other purchasers with a review or star rating and share it with your friends!

CPSIA information can be obtained
at www.ICGtesting.com
Printed in the USA
LVHW022355301219
642052LV00001B/165

9 781989 080382